Catskinner's Book

a novel

by

Misha Burnett

mishaburnett.wordpress.com

ISBN: 9781479179732
PS3602 U7633 C38 2012

Printed in the United States of America

Chapter One

"there is more than one way to skin a cat, but they all end the same for the cat."

The sign in the window says Quality Electrical Supply. If you wander in when we're open—Ten AM to Six PM, Monday through Friday—I could actually sell you some electrical supplies—wire, wire nuts, conduit, junction boxes, breakers, things like that, as long as you didn't need anything oddball.

I do have a number of big catalogs under the counter. I have plenty of time to look through them, but there isn't a lot of point since we don't do special orders. Victor, the owner, doesn't like it.

Quality Electric is off the beaten path, at the corner of two residential streets, next to an empty space that used to be a corner market and then sold liquor and cell phones until the owner got himself shot.

Now there are just some anonymous cardboard boxes covered with dust, a padlocked freezer, and a bunch of office chairs next door. I snagged one of the office chairs for behind my counter, to replace the metal folding one I used to have. If anybody asks for it I'll give it back, but I'm pretty sure no one ever will.

We don't do any advertising at all, not even a line ad in the Yellow Pages. Despite that, we do get some customers, mostly homeowners from the neighborhood who need to replace an outlet or install a ceiling fan. They come in and look around with a sort of half hopeful, half confused expression, like they're expecting to see a shelf labeled, Hey, Joe, This Is The Part You Need!

If I can, I help them figure out what they want, and if I have it I sell it to them. Sometimes they just have questions and I always make sure to tell them that I'm not a qualified electrician. I do know a lot about wiring though. I know a lot about things I'm not supposed to know about.

Sometimes I daydream about making it into a real business, getting an ad in the *South Side Journal*, building up the inventory, maybe a nice display of light fixtures, the kind of faux brass and stained glass stuff that looks vaguely Victorian. Rehabers eat that stuff up. There's a lot of rental property in this neighborhood. I could offer commercial accounts. I'm not saying I'd put Home Depot out of business, mind you, but I bet I could make the place turn a profit.

Of course, the owner doesn't care about selling breaker boxes and GFCI outlets, and he definitely doesn't want people coming in off the street and looking around, so it's just a daydream. It does help pass the time, though, in between the jobs I do for him that actually do make a profit.

Behind the counter there are three doors. There's the one that leads to this weird shaped little space that you could call either a big closet or a small storeroom. It's one of those rooms that no one planned to build, just kind of a leftover from remodeling. I keep a safe in there, but it would be really awkward to try to use it as a stockroom, so it's probably for the best that I don't have any stock. What's on the shelf is what we've got.

The second one is the bathroom thing—it would probably make a better storeroom, but the toilet and sink are in there. It's too big for just a bathroom, though, so it tends to gather all the stuff that I don't know what else to do with. A snow shovel, the folding chair that used to be behind the counter, a filing cabinet that'll come in handy if I ever have anything that needs to be filed. And my coffeemaker, since the sink's in there.

The third door leads to the hall. There's the back door of the building, the back door to the ex-market next door, and Victor's office. He almost never leaves his office, and I don't go back there unless I have to, so I might as well be alone in the building.

Except for Catskinner, of course.

There are apartments upstairs, but the only one that's occupied is mine. You can't get there from the shop, you have to go outside and go back into the building from the alley. When I first moved in I thought that was inconvenient, but now I kind of like it that way. When I lock up the shop at night there's a nice feeling of going home, even though the commute is only twenty feet.

There's an intercom under the counter with the other end in my boss's office. I put it in myself, actually. I did most of the work setting up the shop. Victor would have been happy with an empty room and one bare light bulb. I had to explain that a cover business is supposed to, you know, provide some cover.

So I got a counter, and some shelves, and enough stock to cover the shelves, and a computer I can use as a cash register, but I use mostly to watch music videos on YouTube, and little bell that rings on the rare occasion that someone comes in the front door.

If someone was watching the place they'd know pretty quick that we don't do anything close to enough business to keep the lights on, much less pay my salary, but why would someone watch the place? We don't have enough foot traffic to be dealing drugs, and I keep the sidewalk clean.

I was eating lunch—there's a little pizza place a couple of blocks away with really good sandwiches and free delivery—when Victor buzzed me.

I set down my sandwich, locked the front door, and turned around the **We're Open** sign to the **Back In Ten Minutes** side, and went down the hall.

My boss's office door is metal and it's very heavy. Partly it's because he wants to keep people out, but mostly it's because it's insulated. He likes it cold in his office. Really cold. Outside it was the end of May, and I kept the windows open in my apartment, but in Victor's office it was always darkest February.

I waited until he pushed the button that made the lock go ka-chunk—I didn't wire the electric lock, he called a real electrician for that—and then I pushed it open.

"Hello, Victor," I said. He's fat and he smells awful. His skin is ugly, too, yellow and dry and cracked. Anyone who took one look at him would know that there has to be something seriously wrong with him. I don't mind, though, except for the cold. There's something seriously wrong with me, too—it just doesn't show on the surface.

"Hello, James." He smiled. He's always friendly when he talks to me, and he smiles a lot. His teeth are mostly black.

I sat carefully in the chair in front of his desk. The wood back was fine, but the cloth seat always seemed damp. But it was either that or sit on the big floor safe—he only had two chairs, and he was sitting on the other one.

"How are you doing, James?" Victor asked. There was really only one reason he called me back to his office, and it wasn't to make small talk, but he always asked how I was doing.

I shrugged. "Okay. Good, I guess."

Victor nodded. "You look good. You look like you've put on some weight."

I nodded. "Yeah, probably." I'd always been scrawny, but working for Victor gave my life some stability, including regular meals like the meatball sub waiting for me on the counter.

I wasn't going to ask how he was doing. Not that he'd tell me in detail, anyway. My words came out in little puffs of cloud when my breath hit the cold air. His didn't.

"I think I'll do a little shopping on Saturday. Maybe look for a new stereo." I hadn't been thinking any such thing, but I had to say something. "Okay if I take the van?"

"Of course, of course, any time." Victor grinned at me. "Just make sure you gas it up." Victor always made sure that the company van had a full tank of gas. Why, I wasn't sure. It's not as if he ever drove anywhere.

I nodded, then rubbed my arms. Maybe if I reminded him how uncomfortable his office was he'd get to the point.

It worked. "Well," he said brightly, "it looks like we've got a little job for our friend tonight."

Suddenly I could feel Catskinner's attention from my back. He likes Victor's little jobs.

Catskinner isn't really on my back, because he's not really anywhere—he doesn't have a physical body, so he doesn't have a location in space the way that physical objects do—but that's where the tattoo is, so that's where I always feel him. When he talks to me it sounds like he's standing right behind me, even though I know his voice is just in my head and nobody else can hear him.

Victor handed me a picture, an older man, bald, nondescript in a kind of generic white guy way.

remember him, Catskinner prompted me, even though I was already studying the photograph. He can't recognize humans from pictures of faces, so he relies on me to identify our targets.

I felt my mouth go numb and heard Catskinner using my voice to speak to Victor.

"*just him?*"

"He'll have bodyguards. Three, maybe four. Ex-cops or ex-military. Armed."

"*where? when?*"

Victor handed me a paper menu. It was from a Italian restaurant not that far from our shop. "He'll be there at nine tonight."

"*dinner out,*" and I felt Catskinner laugh. It feels like bugs running up and down my backbone, "*lots of other customers. . . .*"

Victor looked serious. "Only if you have to—and I mean really have to. We want this to be as clean as possible."

Silently I said, Do you want me to get locked up again? and the laughter stopped. Catskinner's bound to my body, and if I'm locked up, he's locked up. Granted, he can make my body do things that ordinary humans can't do, but he can't fly or walk through walls, and if I'm drugged into unconsciousness, he can't see through my eyes or hear through my ears. I spent most of my childhood in and out of institutions until I got big enough to live on my own without arousing suspicion.

I've never been certain, but I think that when I die he'll go back to wherever he came from. In any event, he takes my personal safety very seriously, and it's not from compassion—he's proved many times that he doesn't have any.

"He says he'll be good." I told Victor. I hoped he would be.

Then I went back to finish my sandwich. The job wasn't until late that evening, so I wouldn't have to close up early. I don't like to close up early.

When I unlocked the front door there was someone standing outside. Female, tall, lean, in the way that vegetarian marathon runners are lean, all tendons and bones like a greyhound. Jeans, work boots, and a T-shirt that advertised the Botanical Garden. Short black hair. She looked like she was probably rewiring her house as a revolutionary deconstruction of the patriarchal paradigm.

I unlocked the door and stifled an urge to say, Good afternoon, little missy. I know, I'm a bad person. But I'm okay with that.

Instead I said, "I'm sorry—," as she pushed past me into the store. Catskinner bristled at that. He doesn't like people getting close to me. She smelled like old sweat and some incense— sandalwood, maybe.

"—I was busy in the back," I continued as she stalked right into the middle of the store—three or four steps for most people, two long strides for her—and began scanning the shelves all around

"Is there something I can help you with?" I was starting to feel like I was invisible and she thought the wind blew the door open or something. Also I was acutely aware of the other half of my meatball sandwich sitting on the counter and the fact that I wasn't eating it.

She looked at me then, stared hard at me with a scowl on her face, like she needed something bad and I wasn't it.

Okay, so I'm short and skinny and my hair is kind of muddy brownish and I keep it buzzed because it won't stay flat otherwise—I'll admit I'm nobody's idea of a dreamboat. Still, I was showered and my clothes were clean—that should have counted for something.

I moved over next to the shelves. "Do you need something?"

"I need to know who you are." She was still looking at me like I was the wrong part for some job.

"James Ozwryck." It's pronounced AWE-sig, by the way. No one ever gets it right.

She took a step closer to me. "And who else?"

Catskinner said, *get rid of her now or i will.*

"Nobody else." I deliberately didn't mention Victor. Victor was very much not available for visitors, ever. Catskinner's attention was making me very nervous—he didn't make empty threats, and if he got rid of her it could cause problems. Especially if she had any next of kin.

I was trying to come up with a polite way to say, Go away, you're creeping me out, when she just turned around and left.

Someone even more socially maladroit than I am—I don't run across that very often.

When she closed the door behind her I saw that I'd forgotten to turn the sign around, so I flipped it over to the **We're Open** side. I didn't see the tall woman on the street anywhere.

What's wrong with her? I wondered.

she's still breathing, Catskinner answered, *i could fix that for her.*

That didn't help. His comments usually don't.

Outside the glass door a big panel truck rumbled by, the sides covered with that new plastic film that makes vehicles into billboards.

The Land Of Tan! it advertised, garish letters over a model lying back on a tanning bed, I assumed, although it looked more like an alien life support pod. The woman was tan, of course, blond and busty and wearing an open mouthed smile, white sunglasses, and a green string bikini that covered only what the law required.

I was pretty sure that the tall woman wasn't driving that. It didn't seem her style. Besides, the shadow in the front seat seemed a lot shorter.

The rest of the afternoon was quiet, as usual.

I kept thinking about that woman. The plastic one on the side of the van, not the real one who had stomped through the shop. All of my woman had been plastic, imaginary. Catskinner wouldn't allow anyone to get close to me, and even when he wasn't controlling me he left some kind of mark on me, something that kept people from wanting to get close to me. Except Victor.

I wondered what it would be like to be with a woman like the model on the van. To touch her, to kiss her, to see her lie back and smile at me like she was smiling in that photograph. What would it be like to be able to get close to a woman like that without being scared that Catskinner would hurt her, kill her? Thoughts like that were useless. It didn't stop me from thinking them though.

I finished my sandwich, messed around on-line, and closed up at six. I made myself a pot pie—nothing too heavy—and watched TV for a while.

My apartment isn't much, one long room with a corner walled off as a bathroom and a sort of kitchen built into one wall. I could have more. I could knock out the walls and have the whole second floor. Heck, I could rent an apartment or even a house someplace else—I've got plenty of money these days.

My little place is all I want, though. It suits me, and it's mine. It has a door that I can lock and unlock whenever I want. I have my fridge and all the food I want, my books, my TV and my game console, a good computer, my bed and my clothes. It's a small life, scale model of how ordinary people live.

It's the best place I've ever had.

I like watching old TV shows, and now that a lot of television is available on-line I can catch up on all the shows I missed. I watched a couple of episodes of CSI. I love that show, the characters are likable and the mysteries all have answers. Catskinner seems to like it, too. He laughs a lot, usually during the autopsy scenes.

Then I filled my pockets with candy bars and went to work. At eight-thirty that evening I was getting out of a cab a couple of blocks away from the place Victor had told me about.

The restaurant was a little Italian place. It smelled good, and I wondered how their food was. I'd never eaten there, and after work tonight it would probably be a really bad idea to go back. I could feel Catskinner like a hot towel draped over my back. When he's fully alert it's like the tattoo on my back is made out of wire and the current gets turned up all the way.

I went in the front door. There was a big dining area to the left and a small one to the right. The man I was looking for was on the right. I focused my eyes on him and whispered in my head.

target acquired, he whispered back. He really enjoys our night jobs. I just get out of his way and try not to watch when he's working.

I walked past the host at the podium by the door.

"looking for someone," my mouth muttered.

Only one table in the small section was occupied. There were four men sitting there—the bald man who looked older and more out of shape than he had in Victor's picture, and three younger ones. All of them were wearing jackets and my eyes scanned them as Catskinner looked for weapons.

I had no jacket, no obvious place to hide a weapon, and like I say, I don't look like much. That let me get within a few feet of the table before one of the young men started to get up. He was saying something when Catskinner reached down into all those strings running down my spinal cord and yanked.

My body hopped up on the table. I could feel what my body was doing, the muscles pulling in my legs and the smack of my feet on the tabletop, but Catskinner was in total control and I didn't have to do anything except stay out of his way. The men at the table were all busy, ducking, reaching for things, shouting, and Catskinner kicked out, left and right, knocking plates of food and glasses in their faces.

Then he kicked the bald man in the head. His head spun the side and I felt something crack in his neck. Catskinner kicked him again and now his head was pointed up and to the side. One more kick and his head was turned around almost all the way backwards. His body jerked and salad went all over his lap.

The other men were getting up, shaking off the food and plates. Catskinner gave a jump and the table toppled across two of the men's laps. He rolled off the table as it fell and had a knife in my hand, a wooden handled steak knife he'd gotten off the table somehow. My arm snapped out and then the steak knife was sticking out of the face of the man who wasn't under the table. He slid off the booth onto the ground.

One of the other men had a gun out then, still pushing the table off him. Catskinner reached out and grabbed the gun. He twisted and I could hear the man's fingers breaking. He took the gun and threw it at the other man who was still tangled in the tablecloth.

Catskinner dropped to the floor and bounced back up, and there was a bottle of wine in my hand. He slammed it against the table edge so it broke, wine and glass spraying all around, and pushed the half he was holding into the neck of one of the men and there was a lot of blood.

The last man, the one with the broken hand, was just sitting there, holding his hand, his mouth and eyes wide open. Catskinner scooped up a fork and stuck it in the man's mouth, then pushed until something inside the man snapped and the fork went up into his brain.

People in the rest of the restaurant were starting to get up or get under the tables or just standing and getting ready to scream. Catskinner moves a lot faster than people do, so no one really knew what was going on yet.

Let's go, I suggested. The four men were dead, and Victor said don't do anything with the other customers unless we had to. If we left now we wouldn't have to.

but i like this place, he whispered back, laughing. *love the atmosphere.*

Victor said clean, I reminded him. I could feel the fever in him, the hunger to destroy. I'd be lying if I said that I didn't feel it, too. It felt good, the power, the rush of knowing that the most dangerous thing in the room was under my skin. Catskinner could kill everyone in this building before anyone could stop him, except for me.

Please, I said in my head. Enough. Let's go.

Catskinner turned, slow enough that the other people could see him move. *"goodnight, sweet ladies, goodnight"* he said out loud with my voice, and then we were out the front door, the glass cracking as he slammed it behind me.

Catskinner ran then. Across the street, down an alley, over a fence, down another alley, so fast that I wasn't sure where we were until he slowed down and stepped out onto a street I knew, a couple of miles from the Italian restaurant. And then—just like that—he let go of me and I was walking on my own again. I wasn't tired or sweaty or even breathing hard. I was hungry, though. Ravenous.

Catskinner gets the energy to move my body the same place I do, from the chemical energy stored in my body fat, and this little job had probably burned a thousand calories. Hence the candy bars.

There was a bus stop on the corner, I walked down there and waited for the bus.

Yeah, I know. A contract killer taking the city bus as a getaway vehicle from the scene of a multiple homicide sounds pretty crazy, right?

In the first place, though, no one was going to expect me to flee on foot, and in the even firster place if they did they'd concentrate their search much too close to the scene—Catskinner can cover ground in a way that no police department in the world is prepared to believe. Cabs keep records, and stolen cars can be traced. The bus is a very anonymous way to leave a murder scene—not that I'm advocating murder, mind you. It's not a business that suits everybody.

Besides, there are any number of well-paid expert witnesses willing to testify that I am crazy. Some of whom still have the scars to prove it.

So I sat on a bench with an ad for a pawn shop and ate chocolate for a while. It was a nice evening for sitting on a bench and watching the traffic go by. I did a little discrete checking for blood on my hands and clothes. Didn't see any. Catskinner is a very neat monster. I didn't see a single emergency vehicle go by. Some sirens, but they were far away. The bus rumbled up and I took it close enough to home to walk the rest of the way.

I could have stopped by Victor's office and reported the success of the job—I don't believe he has actually slept for several years—but I didn't feel like it. He'd assume everything went well unless he read otherwise in the on-line papers in the morning.

I went straight upstairs. I wanted to watch TV, maybe find some cartoons where the violence didn't leave scars and everything turned out okay in the end.

The last kill was staying with me, little details coming up every time I tried to close my eyes. That man looked at me, clutching his ruined hand and knowing that he was facing something he could not understand, knowing that he was going to die. He looked at me, and I wasn't there. There was nothing human in my eyes, only Catskinner's hungry alien intelligence. I saw what he saw, mirrored in his dying eyes, a man-shaped hole in the world.

Maybe he was a mafia enforcer, maybe he was a really bad man.

But he had been a man, a human being, and he was dead because something dark and cold and unnatural had used my body as a conduit to reach down onto this Earth and snuff out his life.

Guilt makes me angry. I never asked to be born, never asked to be made into what I am. I'd suggest you take it up with my parents, but they're dead and I devoutly pray that they are suffering more in hell than anything I could ever do to them.

Redemption is costly. Whiskey, on the other hand, is cheap. I took a couple of shots and thought about something else. Bunny rabbits. Puppy dogs. Pretty girls.

Anther couple of shots and I was able to sleep.

Chapter Two

"nature abhors a vacuum. the feeling is mutual."

The next morning—Friday, actually—I woke up hungry. I usually do on days after Catskinner's been active. I took a shower and checked myself over for injuries. Sometimes they don't show up right away, but there was nothing. None of the men last night had so much as touched me.

When I got out of the shower, my coffeepot had finished gurgling, so I poured a cup and made breakfast. Eggs and cheese and toast. I took it out on the back fire escape and ate it while watching the world wake up, well, actually there wasn't a lot of waking up going on in the alley behind the shop. Every once in a while I heard a bus go by.

Four more dead by Catskinner's hand. I wondered if maybe it was time to move on. There was nothing to tie me directly to this killing, and the eyewitness accounts would be useless. The witnesses would be confused and unsure themselves what they saw, and the police would keep working over the stories until they had something that made sense. Looking for something that made sense meant they weren't looking for me.

Still, they could get lucky, and the longer I operated in this area the better their odds got.

Victor would be a problem. He probably could move, but it'd be tough. We'd need a refrigerated truck, probably, and have to have something set up on the other end. It was too complex for me. I could tell him that I was planning on moving and then let him make his own arrangements, but what if he didn't want to go?

What if he didn't want me to go? Could he stop me? Could he stop Catskinner?

I really had no clear idea of Victor's capabilities. If I was going to leave him it would best to just go, disappear into the night. I was good at that.

But, dammit, I liked this town. I liked my little house.

How about it, I asked, should we move on?

all places are the same place.

Yeah. No help there. I finished my breakfast and decided not to make a choice. Instead I washed dishes.

I opened the shop at ten. As soon as I was in, Victor called me on the intercom.

"How did it go?"

"Great," I told him. "Just peachy. A bunch of dead guys face down in their fettuccine alfredo."

A pause. Then, "Are you feeling okay?"

I sighed. "Yeah. Just tired. You know he gets me wound up—it was hard to get to sleep."

"Well, if you want to close up. . . ."

And do what, I wondered? Get drunk and maudlin and think about being a monster? At least in the shop I could pretend that I was doing something useful. "Naw, I'm fine."

"Well, if you want to talk, you know I'm here."

"Thanks," I said. Talk about what? I was suddenly quite sure that if I did move on, I wouldn't tell Victor.

I got on my computer, loaded the music program with a bunch of Tom Waits and Nick Cave. It was that kind of day, Friday or not.

I played some games of solitaire, moved some of the stock around so I could dust the shelves, wrote a couple of checks to pay for the stock I bought last month, and played solitaire some more. I kept losing the card games, which should have told me something, but I've never been good at auguring omens.

The skinny woman came back at noon. This time she had friends with her.

Of course, at first I didn't know that. At first she had nothing but an index card with her. She came through the door and I smiled because I always smile when I see customers, and then I recognized her and my smile kind of faltered and by then—since she's such a long-legged bitch—she was right up to the counter and she whipped out this index card and said, "Would you look at this please?"

and

everything

stopped.

It was a simple 3x5 index card, the kind you use for jotting down addresses or recipes if you're the kind of person who jots down things, one side with lines on it and the other side blank. She held the side that had been blank towards me, but it wasn't blank, it had four characters on it arranged in a diamond, not English. Maybe Hebrew?

I had plenty of time to study them because my body froze. I stood and looked at the card. She nodded a kind of I-thought-so nod, said, "Please keep looking at this," and walked—my head and then my body and then my legs followed her—over to the wall. She put the card against the wall and stuck a push pin through the card into the drywall.

I looked at the card. Four Hebrew letters in a diamond.

She walked to the door and opened it. More people came into the shop but I couldn't look at them. I was looking at the card and the letters. Things were happening behind me. I couldn't turn around. I couldn't move at all.

Doors opened and then footsteps moved down the hallway. There was a bang bang bang, metal on metal, and I heard Victor on the intercom, small and far away, asking questions.

I looked at the card.

In the distance the pounding continued, and then there were crashes and a puff of cold air and a long burbling scream ending in a liquid thud like someone dropping a watermelon on asphalt and a collection of clattering, rifling, and smashes and grabs, all in a doubled echo through the hallway walls and over the intercom, and

I looked at the card.

There was the high-pitched whine of a drill that went on for a long time. I guessed they were opening Victor's safe.

Footsteps coming down the hallway passing behind me and out the door, the little bell ringing impotently at each exit and they were gone.

I smelled old sweat and sandalwood. She was close enough that I could hear her breathing. I waited for her to kill me like she'd no doubt killed Victor, but she didn't. She stood there behind me and then just turned and left.

I was alone.

Looking at a cheap 3x5 card pinned to the wall with a red headed push pin. The air grew cold around me, the door to Victor's office open, probably broken down. It wasn't as cold as it should have been, though. Victor's air conditioner—refrigerator, really—must not be working.

I heard a vehicle start up in the street. A big one. I thought of a blond model in a green string bikini. The Land Of Tan.

Time passed.

My eyes were locked in place, my muscles as cold and unresponsive as carved wood. I knew the feeling well, it was the way I felt when Catskinner took over my body. I reached back into my head and tried to talk to him, Hey, what's going on, What are you doing, Hello, are you there?

Nothing. Dead silence.

Four Hebrew letters in a diamond. They meant nothing to me.

I watched the sunlight fade. I wondered if they had locked the front door when they left. I wondered if they had flipped the sign over. Not that it made any difference. Most days went by without a customer. If customers had come in, though, I wonder what they would have done when they saw me standing and silently staring at a card pinned to the wall. Called 911? Cleaned out the till and walked out? Maybe if someone had waved a hand in front of my face it would have broken whatever hold those characters had on Catskinner. But nobody came in. From time to time I heard cars passing on the street outside.

It grew dark, darker than it should have. The overheads in the shop must be out, I thought, probably they tripped the breakers when they trashed Victor's office.

Victor.

Victor was the only one who had ever really understood what had been done to me. He was the only one who really understood Catskinner. Other people tried to convince me that he was a part of my mind that was split off, that he was a protection mechanism or a coping strategy or something. I got good at agreeing with people who held the keys to the boxes I slept in, but I never believed it.

Catskinner can do things that I can't do. He knows things I have no way of knowing. He doesn't feel pain or fear or compassion or guilt or any human emotion. He sees the world differently than I do. He looks through my eyes but he sees alien relationships, lines of force and consequence that I can't see or understand. He's not alive, not organic. Catskinner can take over my body and use it as a weapon, but he has no more in common with human beings than a stone.

Victor understood that. He knew what Catskinner is in a philosophical sense. He never forgot that, and he never confused the two of us.

He taught me how to give Catskinner the two things he needs—freedom and the opportunity to kill—and how to live free myself.

Victor had been the closest thing to a friend I had ever had.

I was working the door at a strip club in East St. Louis when Victor found me. I had come to an uneasy truce with Catskinner that began when I stood on the edge of a railroad bridge. I'd had enough of running, of hiding, of living like an animal. I couldn't take living with him inside me anymore, never knowing when it would strike out at someone. I was ready to die—death was all I had ever known. It was easy.

Of course he took over my body and stopped me from stepping off the edge, but he must have realized then that he could keep me from killing myself, but he couldn't make me stay alive. He can't control my body all the time—his metabolism is too extreme, and there is too much that he can't do. He moves my body, he can speak with my voice, but he doesn't understand how to live with human beings. He needs me, my cooperation, if he wants to stay out of some maximum security institution.

And he wants very much to be free.

It was easier after that. He began to listen to me, let me tell him when it was safe to hunt and when he needed to stay quiet. Victor taught me how to negotiate better, how to get more of the life I wanted and to be more than just Catskinner's puppet. He recognized what I am the first time he saw me, and we talked that night, very late. Victor's condition wasn't so extreme back then— he could still mingle with ordinary people and pass as one of them. Better than I could, in fact.

I started working for him that week, and he began to find jobs for Catskinner to do. Names and places, people to kill. He gave me some money, but I'm sure he made much more.

Sure, Victor used me, he used both of us, but it was a mutual relationship. Given the choice, I'll take being used over being hunted.

Now Victor was dead. There hadn't been a sound from the back of the store since the tall woman and her companions had left.

Hours, certainly. The only measure of time I had was the shadows on the wall. I was frozen, numb, while the room grew darker. It was surely past the time I would have closed up the shop. On another night I would be upstairs by now, reading or watching television or playing games.

All that was gone now. Whatever happened next, my scale model life died with Victor. I would have to leave, live on the move again, and I'd have to leave my things behind. You have to travel light when you don't know where you're going.

I couldn't stay here without him. I didn't know his contacts. I didn't know how to do his deals. Some of those contacts might come looking for him. I didn't know what he owed to whom, and who might come to collect.

I didn't even know why he died or who killed him. The only one I even saw was the tall woman who nailed Catskinner to the wall with a push pin through a card.

The index card was just a blur, light gray on dark gray, with some squiggles on it, and suddenly I was free.

The pain was like nothing I had even known before. I hit the ground, every muscle in my body cramping and curling me into a ball. My eyes burned and in the darkness I saw clouds of blue roiling across my vision. I tried to close my eyes. I couldn't tell if they obeyed. I could hear myself whimpering. My bowels let go, I felt thick wet warm down my legs. I lay in it and fought to breathe.

the seal of solomon. i had not thought humans yet lived who could construct it.

My cheeks were wet. Tears. My eyes burned. I didn't try to open them, didn't try to move a muscle. I was trembling, all over, so hard it felt like the floor was moving.

Everything ends, in time. Even this.

I don't how long I lay there before it didn't hurt to breathe. I tried moving my hands and they obeyed, still feeling numb and strange. I got them to belt and my zipper, fighting the wet fabric, and crawled out of my jeans. I was sobbing and I still couldn't see—I didn't know if that was the dark or if my eyes were damaged. I got to my knees, reached up and felt up the wall until I felt that index card. I pulled it down. Even though I couldn't see a thing, I pressed my face against the wall and tore it in half, then again, and again, and again, until there was nothing left but pieces too small for my numb fingers to hold.

Enough? I asked Catskinner in my head.

quite sufficient.

I crawled to the counter and used it to pull myself up. I started to see dim shapes against the black. I managed to stagger into the bathroom and slapped the light switch from habit. It didn't come on. Of course. I tried to remember if I had a flashlight. I had a lighter in my jeans pocket, but I wasn't going to go back for it. I washed as best as I could, in the sink, in the dark, and then I drank deep from the tap. It felt good in my mouth, I could feel the dry tissues soaking up the moisture, but it triggered more cramps and I jackknifed forward and vomited it on the floor, water first and then everything else that had been in my stomach.

Strangely, I felt better when the cramps subsided. My limbs had stopped trembling, though I still felt too weak to tackle the stairs to my apartment. I would though. I was going to survive.

Survival was always what I did best.

The breaker box was in the storeroom. The whole place had been built around Victor's cooling equipment, there were shunts and interlocks to make sure that everything else would lose power before Victor's office did. I left the sixty-amp ones alone and slapped the others back on, and I had lights in the shop and hallway. I could finally get a good look at what had been done.

Victor was a mess. He'd . . . liquefied while I had been frozen in the shop. His skin was mostly intact, like a deflated balloon of sickly pale yellow leather. Inside it I could see the lumpy shapes of clustered bones. The rest of what had been him soaked the carpet, thick black and oily, shot through with ropey strands of fiber.

His office was mostly intact though. His big floor safe was open, a neat hole drilled through the face, a lot farther from the lock than I would have expected. I pushed the door open. Inside it was all one big space, mostly empty. Scraps of wire and broken glass littered the bottom.

It had been in there, then, whatever had been worth breaking in here for.

What do I do with him? I wondered.

burn the building down, Catskinner suggested.

It was a good suggestion, but I couldn't do it. Not with all my things upstairs. Not yet. I didn't know what to do. I sat in the hallway, my back against the wall to Victor's office so I didn't have to look at the stain on the floor that used to be the only person I trusted, and I thought about the Sundance Option.

Remember the last scene in *Butch Cassidy and The Sundance Kid?* The Bolivian army has a couple of hundred soldiers set up all around this village square and when Redford and Newman come out shooting, all you can hear is gunfire as the closing credits roll. I've thought about doing that—not going to Bolivia—just walking up to a cop and punching him in the face. Someplace with a lot of other cops around, outside a courthouse, maybe. Catskinner could kill a lot of them, dozens, probably. But in the end they would call out snipers and bring him down.

Suicide by cop, they call that. It would take longer with me, because they wouldn't be expecting one unarmed man to be able to do so much damage. All it would take, though, is one good bullet and they've got thousands.

How about it? I thought, Want to go out in a blaze of glory?

no.

I'm scared. I had a good place here, I was comfortable and I was safe and I had a little house and books and games and I don't want to lose everything again. I don't want to have to run and hide. I don't know what to do, and I'm so tired.

repair the damage. eliminate the threat.

I don't know how.

locate the thieves. kill them. i will kill them. i will make you safe.

I'm so tired.

sleep. i will watch.

And Victor?

move your belongings. burn the building. we don't need him.

So much work.

work tomorrow. sleep now.

I rinsed my pants in the sink until I could stand to get back into them long enough to go down the alley and back upstairs to my apartment. Then I stripped everything off and got in the shower. I was shaking again. Hunger, probably. I needed to eat, but I needed to get clean first.

I microwaved a pot pie, ate it, and then another, and then another. While I was waiting for the microwave I ate chocolate. By the time I finished the third I was starting to feel full, and as the hunger faded, fatigue took its place. I was exhausted, body and soul. So much to do.

Sleep. Move. Burn. Locate. Kill.

Starting with sleep. I got into bed naked and still damp, closed my eyes—

tonight rest

tonight the walking meat that has done this will sleep

tonight they cling to the skin of the world

tomorrow they will fall beneath the shadow of great black wings

they will know fear

they will know sorrow

they will know pain

before they die

—and it all went away. For a while.

Chapter Three

"silence is the song in the heart of all things"

The next morning I woke hungry, but feeling good. I lay in bed for a while, thinking about how to spend my Saturday. Then I remembered, and I got out of bed in a hurry.

The stiffness was out of my limbs, and even my eyes didn't hurt. Catskinner must have been working on my body while I slept. I wondered, not for the first time, how far that could extend. I didn't have a single scar, and I've been wounded plenty of times. I was thirty-something, -six, I think, but I looked twenty. Could Catskinner repair aging? Could he make me immortal?

I didn't want to think about that. I got busy instead.

After I ate I went downstairs and into the shop, but I didn't unlock the door or turn the sign around. I thought about putting a note in the window—closed for family emergency, or something— but it was Saturday and we wouldn't have been open today anyway. I'd be long gone by Monday. Besides, it was probably best not to advertise that I wasn't dead. Just in case.

I had about thirty thousand in cash, mostly hundreds and fifties, in the safe behind the counter. I hadn't expected that much. I'd deposit it a little at a time into my personal checking account, as I needed it. Hauling out wads of cash for major purchases makes people remember you. I had a little toolbox behind the counter, and I dumped the tools and put most of the cash in there.

Before I loaded the van I took out the spare tire and wedged the toolbox next to the jack, then put the tire back in. It didn't sit exactly flat, but it was close enough.

Upstairs I took a look around. No sense in bringing the furniture. It had all come with the place and I could always get more. I unplugged my computer and game box and my stereo. I decided to leave my TV, it was big and old. I could get a flat one when I found a new place to settle in.

I got a box and started filling it with books, movies, music, and games. I ended up putting my towels in the top half so it wouldn't rattle. Toothbrush, razor, and clippers out of the bathroom.

I moved it all down to the van, then went back upstairs and got my clothes. Mostly jeans and work shirts. Socks and underwear. I had two pairs of shoes, and I was wearing one of them.

When I was done the van was less than half full, so I went into the shop. I got the shop computer from the front counter, and my coffeemaker. A few more books from behind the counter. What else? I didn't need the hardware catalogs. I left the stock—such as it was—on the shelves.

A calender on the wall, a desk blotter, an address book, all from distributors, all with places to write down important information. All unused. I guess I didn't have anything important to write down. A poster on the wall showing different kinds of outlets. A mat on the floor that said Come Back Soon!

Even I couldn't see anything in the shop to link me to the place.

I loaded the odds and ends, then went to Victor's office. It seemed strange to see the door open. It was still cool in the room. There was . . . less of Victor than there had been last night. What was left of him had soaked into the carpet, or maybe evaporated. Maybe both. The wooden chair was on its side in the corner, far from the spreading mass that had been my boss. Carefully I stepped over to it and set it upright and sat down. The funny thing was that it didn't smell, or at least not much. A faint chemical odor, like rubbing alcohol and model glue.

"Hey," I said softly, "this sure went south in a hurry, huh?"

I shook my head. "I kind of dropped the ball on you, boss. Some kind of screwed up monster I turned out to be."

I stood. "I'm going to find them, and I'm going to kill them. It's not going to do you any good, probably won't make me feel any better, but I figure it needs doing."

I carried the chair out into the hall, and went back in, looked around the room. I couldn't just leave him there, and I had decided not to burn the building down. For one thing, it was brick, and while I'm sure a brick building can burn down, I have no idea how.

But more importantly, fires mean fire engines and police and arson investigators and insurance people—a whole lot of nosy folks poking around in the ashes.

Besides, it was a residential neighborhood and if I did get the place to burn it would probably spread. I may be a monster, but I didn't want to burn somebody's house down by accident.

I'm going to need you to move the desk and the safe, I told Catskinner.

move to where?

Out in the hall. Off the carpet. I'm going to pull up the carpet—it's the only way to get his body up.

I expected him to argue with me, but he just took over long enough to pick up the safe, set it in the hall, and come back for the desk. Then he sank back and let me do the rest.

I cut the carpet away from the walls and rolled it up. There wasn't any way to do it neatly. I ended up with a lumpy bundled that smelled like melted plastic. I carried it into the empty space next door, to the freezer.

Break the lock.

Catskinner didn't comment, just lashed out with my hand and the hasp snapped. The freezer was warm and dry and empty. Victor fit in there neatly. Even with the carpet there wasn't much of him.

Goodbye, Victor. I never really knew you, I never really knew what you were, but you were good to me, for a while. That puts you on a very short list. I'll miss you.

me, too.

The side drawers of Victor's desk were locked, but the long flat one in the center opened easily. A broken watch, a little memo book full of scribbles that weren't English, some rubber bands, a half bag of cough drops, a handful of coins, mostly European, a package of pipe cleaners, a few pens, a red eraser, dried and crumbling. An old Polaroid snapshot of a woman on a bridge looking away from the camera.

I held the picture in my hands, turned it over. There was something on the back, but the ink was too faded to even tell what language it was written in. I considered taking the picture, something to remember him by.

Instead I just turned the breakers back off, took one last look around the place, and locked up.

I drove to my bank, deposited two thousand in cash, then found a self-storage place up north by the airport. After I rented a locker and put most of my stuff in it, I checked into a Residence Inn and paid for a week in advance on my debit card.

I put my clothes away, a couple of books on the bedside table, made a cup of really awful instant coffee. There was a little kitchenette with a fridge and a stove top, I'd buy groceries later.

I sat on the bed for a while, getting a feel for the place.

Home? No. But I was used to that.

I had work to do. Me and Catskinner both.

And I thought I knew just where to start.

There wasn't any Land Of Tan under "Tanning Salons" in the yellow pages, so tried the white pages. One line, **Land Of Tan, The**, with a phone number but no address. Just like **Quality Electrical Supplies**' listing. They probably had the same phone plan that Victor had.

I didn't really have any idea what to do next. Try calling them?

Why not? I got a recorded message saying that the business hours were ten AM to eight PM, Monday through Saturday and to call again later. They didn't give an address. It was just after one on Saturday, so they should have been open. Did that mean they closed up shop after the break-in? Was the Land of Tan set up just as a cover for the break-in? What did Victor have that was so important? Money? Sure, there had probably been a lot in his safe, but enough to make it worthwhile to set up a dummy business to get it? Maybe, maybe a phone number and a van was all they had.

I had too many questions, and no idea how to get the answers. Clearly I needed the Internet.

I'd put both computers into storage, so I drove down and got the one from the shop and brought it back to the motel. I had to go to the office and buy a cord, then spend half an hour restarting the computer until it finally admitted that there was an Internet out there, and if I promised to be good I could look at it.

I found it by accident. I was looking for reviews of local businesses and I couldn't find any listing for tanning salons, so I was clicking away from the page when a coupon popped up for a Mexican restaurant. There was a picture, a sad looking little strip mall, and there next to Pollo Grande was a space with darkened windows and The Land Of Tan written across the awning.

Hello, there. I wrote down the address and looked it up. South County.

I had a place to start, anyway. I could drive down there and—
kill them all

—talk to them, I was thinking. If anyone was there. Look for clues if no one was. Not that I was all that sure what a clue would look like.

Screw it. I had to do something.

The strip mall was even sadder looking in person. There was a laundromat at one end that had a handful of cars parked around it, then a couple of empty spaces, then The Land Of Tan, then

Pollo Grande on the corner. There was a big sign in the lot that proclaimed "Business Property! Great Location!" but it wasn't fooling anyone. I wrote down the phone number. It seemed like a good investigative thing to do.

I parked at the back of the grocery store lot a block away and walked back. There was a lot of traffic on the road—Saturday afternoon, prime shopping time—but no one on foot. It wasn't the kind of neighborhood you walked in, even though it was a beautiful afternoon for walking. South County people.

What if they have another one of those cards, I wondered.

don't look at it.

Great advice. The Mexican place was closed, with a "Visit Us at Our New Location" notice in the window, but no address for the new location. Good thing I hadn't printed out that coupon.

Land Of Tan was closed and locked, the windows tinted with some dark film. It didn't look like there were any lights on inside. The lock on the door was shiny and new and looked like it belonged on a bank vault. Interesting. I decided to walk around and check out the back of the building.

The storefront next to the Land Of Tan had the same dark film on the windows, and the same kind of overdeveloped lock. Also interesting.

The next storefront over was just your basic empty storefront. Big vacant space, clean, but somehow desolate, with that abandoned look that big empty spaces have. Threadbare blue carpet on the floor, brackets for holding shelves but no shelves on one wall, ranks of dusky florescent fixtures—

—I was suddenly facing the street. Catskinner had noticed her before I did. Maybe forty, brown hair with an artful streak of gray in it, short and kind of round, wearing a well-made suit that was tailored to make her look a little less short and a little less round. She had a nice leather briefcase and a warm smile that faltered only a little when Catskinner spun and stared at her.

"Are you Craig?"

With an effort I took my body back, lowered my hands. Let me talk to her.

careful.

Was I Craig? That was an easy one. "No."

"Debbie Sawyer." She reached into her back and pulled out a card. I flinched, but it was just a business card. "I'm the leasing agent."

I took the card. Sure enough, it said, "Debbie Sawyer, Leasing Agent."

She was look at me, an expectant smile on her face, so by reflex I said, "James Ozwryck," then felt like kicking myself. I should have made up a fake name.

"This is a good property, James," she said. "Don't you think so?"

Actually, I thought it was one step above a ruin, but I nodded.

"We'll build to suit, of course, and since we currently have three spaces open, we can offer a number of attractive alternatives."

She thought I was a customer. That was better than thinking I was a burglar. Maybe.

"I'm just looking."

She nodded, seriously. "Well, do you think a space like this would meet your needs? We do have other properties available if you're looking for warehouse space or manufacturing."

I looked around, hoping that Craig would show up and take her away. The lot was empty except for a man over by the laundromat who was leaning on a car, talking on a cell phone and smoking. Somehow he didn't look like a Craig to me.

What would meet my needs is for her to let me into Land Of Tan for a look around. I doubted that would happen, but maybe I could get some information from her.

"I have a little electrical supply house, in South City, and I'm . . . thinking about new locations."

"Expanding?"

"Just moving. I mean, I like the city and all, but—" But what? I was no good at this. I should have worked out some cover story in advance, along with a fake name.

"City sales tax?" she suggested.

Gratefully I nodded.

"Sure, that's part of it, and I'm hoping to expand my, uh, customers, and all that."

I waved at the vacant storefront. "So, uh, could I take a look at the space?"

She looked crestfallen. "I don't have keys to the units with me." Then she brightened. "I'd be happy to make an appointment. The first part of next week?"

"Sure." I found myself setting up a meeting next Tuesday morning. I gave her the phone number for Quality Electrical.

"By the way," I said, "I noticed that the tanning place seem to be closed today. Do you know if they are closing for good? I'd hate to be the only store in the whole mall that was open."

She turned to look at the darkened door. "I really don't know anything about them." Her voice seemed strangely flat. Then she turned back to me. "I should be going." Big smile. "See you on Tuesday."

"Yeah, see you then." I looked around. "I'll just . . . check out the neighborhood."

She headed back towards the street and I went in the direction of the laundromat. There were four cars parked outside it and about that many people inside, sitting and watching their clothes go round. The man who had been outside smoking was inside now, still talking on his phone.

I crossed in front of the doors and went around to side of the building. The wall was cinder block and blank. Someone had spray painted a crude profile of a woman, an exaggerated figure with high heels and oversize circles for breasts. One of her feet pointed backwards, maybe to indicate spread legs.

Behind the strip mall was an alley with a high wooden fence on the other side. I looked through the boards and saw a parking lot full of cars and what looked like a chain restaurant.

I stepped back from the fence and looked around. I could hear cars going by on the street, but they seemed small and far away. I was alone.

I counted out the back entrances to the empty shops, miscounted, and realized I had gone too far when I saw the Mexican restaurant's back door. So the one next to it must be—

dangerous. be careful.

It didn't look dangerous. It looked like the back door of a retail storefront. No name on the door, just a blank metal door with a shiny new knob. Can you open that? I asked in my head.

yes.

My hand took hold of the knob, gripped it tight, and twisted. It resisted, and my hand twisted harder, and then something in it snapped and the knob turned easily. My hand was my own again.

Deep breath. I didn't even know for sure that this place was connected with what had happened to Victor and me. Maybe someone stole the van. Or maybe the van I'd heard on Friday wasn't the same one I'd seen on Thursday. The locks looked suspicious and it was odd that the place was't open today, but that wasn't proof of anything.

To hell with that. I knew in my gut that the people who killed Victor and paralyzed me had something to do with this place. That was good enough for me.

Nothing beeped, buzzed, or blew up when I pushed open the door. It was dark in there and warm, hot, even. The air was humid and smelled . . . organic somehow. Like I walked into a greenhouse. I was in a hallway that stretched the length of the space. At the end I could see hints of sunlight around the edges of the dark film on the window.

The hallway had doors on both sides. There was light—electric light—coming from under one of the doors on my right. It seemed a logical place to start. I closed the door behind me as quietly as I could and stood waiting for my eyes to adjust to the dimness. With the door closed the smell was thicker and sweeter. Orchids and . . . yes, sandalwood. It smelled like the tall woman in the Botanical Garden T-shirt.

I slunk down the hallway. The doors I passed were closed. I didn't hear anything. I grabbed the knob of the door where the light was, took a breath and slammed it open.

Inside was a tiny room. In the center of the room was the tanning bed from the picture on the van. Sitting on the bed—it was open—was the young lady from the picture.

She'd been reading some thick paperback when I burst into the room. She gave a little cartoon squeak and dropped the book. Her bikini top, lips, and sunglasses were matching pink and her blue jean shorts were cut off raggedly at mid-thigh.

Not what I expected. She looked up at me and I looked down at her. I stared. I couldn't help it. Her body was simply perfect, full and rounded and lush and her skin looked so smooth and so soft, glowing with health.

She drew her legs up to her chest, folded her arms around them, hugging herself. Looked up at me.

I had no idea what to say.

"I need answers," I tried. It sounded less threatening and more petulant than I'd intended.

She nodded gravely.

"Uh, look, yesterday some people broke into my shop and killed my boss and took what was in his safe. I think they came from here."

Another nod. Her sunglasses had big round mirrored lenses. Under them her mouth was serious.

"There was this woman, she was tall and thin. She had, uh, dark hair, cut real short."

She spoke then. "There's nobody here." Her voice was both deeper and softer than I expected. There was something strange about the way her face moved when she spoke, as if her jaw stayed closed and only her lips moved. She reached up to settle her sunglasses on her face and I noticed that her fingernails were also that same pink shade.

the human has been compromised.

What do you mean, compromised?

altered. changed. it is no longer entirely human.

She, I corrected Catskinner, not it.

she is also not entirely female.

She looked like a girl to me. What I could see of her face looked young enough that I would have carded her and taken a good hard look at her ID.

"I'm looking for that woman I told you about. Does she work here?"

She nodded. Her tongue darted out and touched her lips. Again I had the feeling that there was something wrong with the way her mouth moved. Maybe that was the change Catskinner meant.

She stretched her legs out. Her toenails were pink, too.

She cocked her head to the side. I got the feeling she was studying me from behind her glasses. She leaned forward. Licked her lips. Looked up at me.

"I'm hungry," she said. "I'll blow you for some food."

Oh, God. This was not going at all how I expected.

Chapter Four

"normal is the name given to the most common miracles"

I was speechless. This kind of thing didn't happen in the real world, did it?

The girl was looking up at me, smiling. Her lips were shiny, and her glasses reflected tiny copies of my dumbstruck face. I looked away, tried to get some composure.

One wall was covered by a huge print, a photograph of a beach scene. It was the pier at Huntington, I'd been there. The girl would have fit in there, lying on a towel, soaking up the sun, laughing and talking with the boys. On the other wall was a poster that detailed how long you could stay in a tanning both before it was dangerous.

A thought struck me. "Did everyone else just go away and leave you here?"

A nod.

"I'll get you some food." I felt myself blush. "You don't have to do—

—*take off your glasses.*" Catskinner interrupted me suddenly.

She recoiled a bit at the sound of Catskinner's voice. Slowly she reached up and took off her sunglasses.

Her eyes were green. Not green like people usually mean that, white on the outside, black in the center, green in the middle. Her eyes were all green, lighter at the edges, darker in the middle. Not human eyes, more like a dog's eyes.

She blinked at the light, lowering her head.

"You can put them back on," I said. "I—what's your name?"

"Godiva," she said.

Godiva. Yeah, sure, why not. "I'm James."

She smiled at that, a small, tight smile, and I saw that she didn't have any teeth, at least in front.

"Okay, Godiva, let's take a look around, and then we can go get some food, okay?"

She hopped up to her feet. Human or not, female or not, her body was distractingly lovely. Standing, the top of her head came up to my chin.

We started at the front door. There was a counter with some brochures about how to get toned, fit, and sexy by giving other people money. There was a space on the counter where a cash register or computer once sat, the shape of the box left in dust. The drawers behind the counter were empty except for a couple of paper clips and a pen that had bled all the bottom of the drawer.

There were a couple of chairs and a low table with magazines and catalogs scattered on it. A bulletin board with a few push pins, a couple of scraps of paper that looked like the corners of fliers, and a few staples. Godiva poked through some of the magazines.

Nothing that looked like a clue to me. It did make me think of something, though. "Godiva, if you see me, uh, freeze up and not move, put your hands in front of my face, okay? See, when they broke into my store they had this card that kind of hypnotized me. As long as I could see it, I couldn't move."

She nodded seriously, just as if that made sense, and went back to looking through the magazines. She grabbed one and held it out to me proudly.

Natural Glamour. On the cover a woman with feathers in her hair looked vacantly at some distant mountains.

"You want that?" I asked her, "You can have it."

"Look," Godiva said, sounding a little exasperated. She pointed at the address label. Dr. Madeline Klein, with an address that wasn't this one. "That's her."

"The tall woman with black hair?" I took the magazine. "Madeline Klein?"

Godiva nodded.

"Thank you," I said, "You're better at this investigation stuff than I am." A name and a home address. Maybe this was working after all.

The hallway was lined with doors. Most of them led to the tanning rooms, pretty much identical to the one where I'd found Godiva. The beds were like exam tables with lids, the lids packed with short florescent tubes. They looked even more like props in a low budget science fiction movie in person, but maybe all tanning beds look like that. There was also one bathroom, which looked just like the tanning rooms, only with a toilet and sink instead of a bed.

The two doors at the end of the hall, closest to the door I'd come in, were different. For one thing, both were locked. The one on my right was no problem, I stuck my pocketknife in between the door and the jam and we were in there. It was an office, only slightly larger than the booths. There was a desk, a wall calender, and a filing cabinet. The desktop was conspicuously bare. I looked through the desk drawers and found a stash of granola bars. I gave them to Godiva.

"I told you I'd get you some food."

She flashed me a grin, wide enough that I could see she was entirely toothless. Somehow, it didn't look bad on her. I wondered, though, if she had worn dentures in the model shop, or if teeth had been photoshopped in.

She seemed to have no problem with the granola bars, she skinned off the wrappers and started devouring them. She turned away from me, looking embarrassed. I respected her privacy and turned to look at the filing cabinet.

Paper clips, rubber bands, a couple of torn off ends of paper that might have meant something to the techs on CSI but were useless to me. Godiva had finished the granola bars—five or six of them—and stood with the wrappers in her hand.

I picked up the trash can by the desk and paused. It hadn't been emptied. There were a handful of empty envelopes in there, incoming mail, slit open at the top. What the heck. I stuck them in my pocket along with the magazine.

The door on the other side of the hallway was another story. It was metal and had the same kind of lock as the back door.

"Do you know what's back there?"

"Dr. Klein's . . . medicine stuff."

"Did she give you medicine? To . . . change you?"

Godiva looked at the ground and nodded, then glanced back at me. I smiled at her. "It's okay," I said. "I'm different, too."

Would you? I asked Catskinner.

gladly.

This time he didn't just break the lock, he kicked the door. The door held, the jam held, the wall gave way and the whole door and frame slammed to the ground. Subtle, it wasn't.

Fortunately there wasn't anything on the other side of the door. I reached to take my body back, but Catskinner wouldn't yield.

"*godiva,*" he said out loud. "*we haven't been introduced. i don't have a name, but james calls me catskinner.*"

"Hello," Godiva said hesitantly.

What are you doing? I asked, trapped in my head.

"*i'm what's different about james. what's different about you?*"

Godiva looked down at the ground. "You don't know?"

I fought harder. He fought me back.

"*i know what. i don't know why.*"

She looked at him—at me, helpless behind my eyes.

"It's for sex," she said, contemptuously. "Something like you wouldn't understand that."

Catskinner released me and I stood there with Godiva glaring at me. I looked away.

"I'm sorry," I said.

"Is it always there?" she asked.

"Yeah," I admitted. "He's not always active, but he's always there. My whole life."

I turned to the door that Catskinner had kicked down. There was a short hall and a larger space, it had to be the vacant storefront next door.

"Your whole life?"

I sighed. "When I was an infant my parents tattooed something on my back. It summoned him and bound him to my body. Like a magic circle or something. I don't know how it works."

I stepped on the fallen door, walked across it to the open area.

Godiva followed me. "Why?"

"I don't know," I said without turning around, "maybe there was nothing good on TV."

There was a good sized chemistry lab in there. One of the long walls had a row of tables against it and the tables were covered with glassware and tubing, a couple of big heavy boxes that could have been centrifuges or could have been toasters for all I knew. The smell was very strong, a mix of compost and spices.

There were a couple of the tanning beds, both of them looking like they'd been partially broken down for parts. There was a lot of the usual junk that seems to accumulate in spaces like this, broken chairs, an aluminum extension ladder, a wheelbarrow, a rolling coat rack with what looked like a random selection of clothes on it, a bank of gym lockers.

Godiva went to the coat rack and started picking through it. I started opening the lockers. The first one seemed to be full of belts, canvas and leather, with big buckles. I went on to the next. There was a dusty lab coat hanging on a hook, a bunch of empty plastic tubes at the bottom.

Godiva joined me at the lockers, starting at the other end. She'd pulled a baggy gray T-shirt on, it made her older, somehow. More respectable.

I found a couple more lab coats and a stack of old, thick books. *Handbook of Chemistry and Physics*, *Common Reactions and Reagents*, *Physicians Desk Reference. Benway's Guide to Endocrinology.* Fun stuff.

"Hey," Godiva called to me. I looked over and she smiled. She had teeth, very white and very shiny. She had a cute smile, but it looked odd, artificial. Maybe that was just because I'd seen her without them.

At the bottom of the next locker was a green metal cash box. I opened it. Cash, a couple of hundred at least. Godiva was at the locker next to me. I handed it to her. She glanced inside, then back at me.

"I figure it's your severance pay."

She clutched the box to her. For a moment she looked very lost. "Can I touch you?"

"Sure," I said and then I realized that she wasn't asking me. Can she?

i don't like it.

I'm not asking you to like it, I'm asking you not to hurt her.

if you must.

"It's okay," I told her. "He won't do anything."

She came to me and put her arms around me, still awkwardly clutching the cash box. Her body was very warm, soft and small. It was like holding a kitten. She pressed her head against my chest and her hair smelled like flowers.

"They're not coming back for me," she whispered into my chest. "They're really not."

"No," I agreed. "I don't think they are."

"I don't know what to do now."

I put my arms around her. I could feel Catskinner's revulsion. I ignored it.

"I don't either." There didn't seem to be anything more to say.

She looked up at me. Her glasses slid down her nose and I met her strange animal eyes.

"Are you going to kill Dr. Klein?"

"If I find her."

"I'll help you find her." Her eyes were shining and she blinked away moisture. She stepped back. It was hard to let her go.

She went back over to the clothes rack and found a black clutch purse. She dumped the cash in it. She took a deep breath and pushed her glasses back up.

"Let's get out of this fucking place."

"Yeah. And let's get some lunch."

She smiled at me, her artificial teeth bright and her pink lips shining.

I could get used to that smile, I thought.

predictable.

Just shut up, okay?

Just before we left, Godiva stopped and held up a hand. "Wait just one minute, please."

I nodded and she ducked back into the both where I had first found her. She came out with a pink Victoria's Secret shopping bag. The book she had been reading was sticking out of the top.

Catskinner tensed. *search the bag*, but it was a suggestion, not an order.

Instead I said to Godiva, "You've been living here?"

She nodded. "Just temporary." She looked down and I wondered how long "temporary" had been, and what she had been doing to pay the rent.

The address on Dr. Klein's magazine was in West County. I pulled up to the first drive thru place we passed and we ordered a lot of food. As we pulled away Godiva sorted through the bags then looked up at me shyly.

"I can't eat with the teeth in," she said quietly.

"Take them out. Nobody will see in."

I didn't look over at her while she was eating. I kept my eyes on the road and snagged a couple of burgers. On the highway she put her hand on my arm and I glanced over at me. She looked serious, her teeth back in place.

"Are you going to kill Dr. Klein now?" she asked.

I sighed. "I don't know. I might. I want to talk to her, see how it goes from there. Hell, she might not even be home."

Godiva looked at me, her eyes unreadable behind her glasses. "I think I should go with you," she said at last in a small voice.

I nodded. I figured she deserved to be a part of whatever happened.

We took 270 around to Ladue road. I had a street guide in the van. Godiva looked up the address. She turned out to be a fine navigator.

"Have you been out here before?" I asked her.

"Not in years," she said, "but I grew up around here." Her tone of voice didn't invite further inquiry.

Dr. Klein's house was an imitation castle on a corner lot with a high privacy fence surrounding most of the property. I parked down the street. I still didn't exactly have a plan, but I trusted Catskinner would take over when the time came.

"You stay in the van," I told Godiva.

i don't trust her.

"Maybe I could help."

It was confusing, both of them talking at once. It wasn't something that I was used to. We have to trust her, I told Catskinner.

Aloud I said, "Probably not—Catskinner's used to working alone. Besides, if anything happens to me, I don't want her to know you were working with me."

"I don't want anything to happen to you." She looked very serious.

I smiled. "Me, either. Don't worry, I'll be fine. You just wait here."

if she doesn't wait?

We'll deal with that if it happens. It was another one of
those neighborhoods where no one walks. They didn't even have
sidewalks.

Police response time is probably pretty quick around here, I
thought to Catskinner.

agreed. best to be quiet.

I could feel the electric heat on my back, his eagerness, his
hunger to destroy. For once I knew how he felt. As I walked up the
driveway I could see the shape of a van in the garage. The Land Of
Tan van. I hope that meant she was home.

The door was a big slab of ornate wood with a stained glass
window in it. Very pretty. I rang the bell.

Are you ready?

it's showtime.

Chapter Five

"there is no right answer to the wrong question"

"Hi there. My imaginary friend wants to skin you alive."

Her reaction was all I could have hoped for. She'd answered the door in an elaborately embroidered robe that looked like silk. She looked stunned to see me. She'd probably thought I would die when she left me pinned to the wall.

For a moment she just stared at me.

"That Solomon trick won't work twice," I said. "My friend doesn't need to see you to kill you."

I stepped inside and she backed away slowly. I shut the door behind me. We were in a two-story foyer with a painted tile floor. Archways were open to the left and right; straight ahead carpeted stairs led up. There was a bookcase against one wall full of little gewgaws and doodads, most of them looking vaguely Aboriginal. Pier One schlock.

"I've got some questions."

She nodded. She looked scared, but not scared enough to talk. Not yet.

"I want to know why you killed Victor—"

"He died a long time ago."

"Shut up," I said. She glared at me, but didn't say anything else.

"I want to know why you killed Victor. I want to know what you took from his safe, and I want it back. After that, we can talk about how you're going to die."

She folded her arms across her chest. "Is that all?" She was starting to look more angry that frightened.

"Yeah, that's about it."

She shook her head. "You have no idea what Victor was, do you? You don't even know what you are."

"Maybe so, but I know what you are."

Oh, really? And what's that?"

Catskinner answered for me. "*skin. muscle. blood. bone.*"

That rattled her.

"My friend's still kind of upset. As I'm sure you know, I can't always control him."

"You can't ever control it, and you never will. You're just a puppet." Her voice dripped contempt.

I shook my head. "If that was true, you'd already be in pieces." In my head I asked, Can you scare her without killing her? I want her to talk.

Catskinner's reply was to lash out to the shelf next to me. Something dark blurred past her head and exploded into pottery shards against the far wall. He grabbed another one and it detonated at her feet. The next one he crushed in my hand and threw a handful of red-brown dust in her face.

Now I was seeing real fear on her face. "Stop it!" she cried out.

Catskinner snatched up a bit of crystal and snapped it against the shelf, shattering it. With one of the shards he thrust forward, cutting her robe across her chest without touching the skin below it. He snapped the shard to one side and it embedded in the shelf.

"*it stops when you talk.*"

"The book!" she shouted at me. "His book was in the safe."

I felt Catskinner pull back.

"Book?" I asked. "What book?"

"The Book of Thoth." She glared at me defiantly.

"Thoth, huh? Egyptian guy, head like a bird or something? That Thoth?" I took another step towards her, she took another step back.

"You don't know anything."

"So tell me, and then I'll know. Where's Thoth's book now?"

"Gone. Dissipated." With a contemptuous glare. I wanted to slap that look off her face.

"So you were just there for kicks, then? Just because you get off on killing people?"

"There were no people there. Unnatural things."

I was starting to lose my temper. "Unnatural? As opposed to what you did to Godiva, which was perfectly natural?"

Damn. I hadn't wanted to mention Godiva. The response was gratifying, though. Her eyes widened and she backed up a few more steps. She hadn't expected me to know about Godiva.

I pressed on. We were by the stairs now. "How do you think I got your address?"

"Godiva wanted it done."

"And that makes it okay to leave her—"

She interrupted me by laughing. "You're an idiot."

"Maybe so, but I know evil when I see it." I walked closer. She backed away through the arch to the left. I could see more of her house now. A conversational grouping, matching chairs and couch, polished blond wood and brown leather. It looked expensive.

"Evil? With that reaver inside you?"

"Reaver?"

i do reave upon occasion.

Thanks, I know.

shall i scare her some more?

Not just yet.

She was looking at me closely, as if she could sense my internal conversation. Deliberately she took two slow steps back. I followed her.

"Where are you going?" I asked sharply.

She spread her hands. "You tell me."

"I like this room. We'll stay right here."

She planted her feet and folded her arms and glared.

She was right about one thing—I didn't know half of what I needed to, and I didn't even know the right questions to ask.

"Who else was with you?"

"Just me and my imaginary friends."

Okay, your turn.

Catskinner lashed out and slapped her across the face, hard enough to knock her off balance. With my other hand he grabbed the front of her robe and yanked. She fell, naked, and Catskinner tossed the torn pieces of the robe behind me.

Now there was real fear in her eyes. She crawled backwards and Catskinner stalked towards her, driving her back to where a plate glass door separated the room from the fenced back yard. Idly I noticed there was a large in-ground pool. Typical.

"you live on an island gathering shells on the shore and you think that you can control the tides because you can reckon their rise and fall. you see the surface of the waves and you think you know the sea."

She scrambled backwards, her eyes wide with panic. She reached the glass door, pressed up against it, Catskinner bent down to put my face close to hers. I could feel his death's head rictus on my face.

"you walk across the skin of this world and you think the ground is solid under foot. you close your eyes when you fall under the shadow of great black wings, and you tell yourself the sun will rise again."

"but you know," –he reached out to brush my fingers across her arms, crossed tight against her chest— *"you know in your heart that one day the sun will set and never rise again. you know the deep that waits for you, in the cold, in the dark, in the stillness, in the forever."*

He straightened, pressed my palms against the glass door. I felt the tension gather in my arms and then the glass exploded outwards.

She screamed and he leaned back down to her.

"hush. just answer the question."

"I don't know their names! Keith arranged it! They were just drones from the Manchester nest!"

Catskinner turned and I felt his control slip away. I turned back. "Thank you, Dr. Klein."

She looked up at me, and I could see the gratitude in her face that she was talking to a human being again. As much as she might hate me, I was better than Catskinner.

The story of my life.

"Now, who's Keith, and what's this Manchester nest?"

I could see her give up. The defiance that had been keeping her face closed and her body tense faded away, ran out of her body like water. Her voice was soft as she spoke.

"Keith Morgan. He runs The Good Earth, on Lindbergh, near highway 40. All the nests buy from him. They say he's in bed with some of the others, the blue metal boys, the nova crew—I don't know about that. I got my nettle junk from him. I just wanted to get out from under and out of town—I swear that's all it was. He gave me the seal and told me how to use it."

I nodded, just as if I understood what she was talking about. So far, her being cooperative wasn't much more help than her being defiant.

You getting all this?

i hear it.

Which meant that it didn't make any more sense to Catskinner than to me. Still, I did have one lead to follow up.

"The Good Earth," I repeated sagely, as if I had expected as much and just wanted her to confirm it. "And the Manchester nest?"

"I don't know the address. It's out past 270, almost to 141. It's in an old department store. That's all I know."

I turned from her and she flinched, but I just gathered up the remains of her robe and tossed it at her. She pulled it gratefully over her body.

I needed time to think. Blue metal boys? Nova crew? They

sounded like gangs of some kind. Was that what happened? We got caught in a gang war?

"So what did Keith have against me and Victor?"

I lost points with that one. I could tell from her expression that it was a stupid question, but she opened her mouth to answer it anyway when there was a fusillade of knocks on the door.

"Police, open up!"

That's our cue to exit.

She was looking towards the door. I smiled and told her, "Getting out of town—that's probably a good idea."

She looked back at me in time to see Catskinner pouring back into my face and body.

"talking about me, now that's a really bad idea."

And then we were gone, over the scattering of broken glass and through the empty door frame, across the patio—I had time to glimpse the water of the pool, green with algae like swamp water—then I was at the privacy fence.

And then Catskinner stopped dead. There was movement on the other side of the fence. The cops had the place surrounded. I could feel Catskinner giving the fence his full attention.

Remember, I urged him, we don't kill cops. Cops never stop looking for someone who kills their own.

In the backyard there was a pool, a couple of plastic chaise lounges, an old wooden tool shed, and me. Catskinner turned my head to look at the pool. It was worse than I thought, the surface was scummed with green and swarms of tiny bugs hung around it like a cloud.

Try the shed, I suggested.

The shed wasn't locked. Once inside I reached to take my body back. Catskinner gave it up easily. I was hungry and hot, but basically okay, although I didn't expect that to last. As soon as Dr. Klein told the cops where to find me I was screwed. Catskinner could get clear of them, I was sure, but probably not without hurting some of them.

I watched through the crack between the doors and waited.

I saw Dr. Klein talking to the cops, still wrapped in the shreds of her robe.

Try not to kill any of them when they come, I whispered in my head.

agreed.

Dr. Klein kept talking, and the cops nodded. Then they started walking away—back into the house, not out into the backyard where she had to know I was. A little while later I heard cars pulling away—no sirens.

I started to let myself hope a little bit. Could it be that Catskinner had frightened her enough that she didn't actually tell them about me? It seemed too much to ask.

On the other hand, he could be really scary.

I didn't see Dr. Klein or the cops anywhere. I eased the door open. No one shot at me, or yelled, or anything.

I stuck my head out. Catskinner was close to the surface, I could feel him just under my skin, but he wasn't trying to take control, just being vigilant.

I think we might be able to make a break for it.

look at the pool.

I looked. There were shapes under the algae, drifting shadows. I tried to make sense of the form, something long and lean, like a shark, but with limbs. Not just limbs, but legs and arms. Not a fish. The shadow resolved itself into a human form, drifting slowly under the scum. Then another. And—

—get us the hell out of here.

Catskinner's will poured into my limbs and then I was at the fence, over the fence, and across the neighbor's yard. I didn't see any police on the side of the house, I hoped that meant they were gone.

It wasn't Catskinner Dr. Klein was scared of. It was what the police would find if she'd sent them out back to get me.

I passed through a handful of lawns dotted with ornamental trees. Catskinner kept my head moving, scanning the streets. No sign of police. No sign of anyone, really. I crossed another yard, out to sidewalk and down to the corner to where Godiva was waiting in the van.

The van wasn't where I left it.

Chapter Six

"silence never lies."

Catskinner realized it before I did. My body slowed and my head swiveled back and forth, scanning the street.

You're going to say I told you so, aren't you?

I felt my lips stretch into a grin.

i did tell you so, actually.

My body slowed to Catskinner's approximation of a normal human walking pace. I didn't try to take back control. I was busy trying to think.

Options? Run in circles, scream and shout? Probably not too productive at this time. Steal a car? Right. The cars in this neighborhood were loaded with all kinds of electronic anti-theft gear that I had neither the training nor the tools to overcome.

Catch a cab? That's a laugh—cabs don't cruise around here. Same with buses, except on the major streets. I needed to get out of the residential area. Keep walking and hope I don't get stopped by the cops.

Not the greatest plan in the world, but it was all I had. I could feel Catskinner's agreement, he eased up into a jog. Good idea, people around here don't walk, but they do jog. Bully for fitness.

The question was, where did Godiva go? If she just cut and ran, I could understand that. I could almost forgive it. She didn't owe me anything, really. She could have gotten out of Land Of

Tan by herself, she might even have gotten the cash (and her teeth) without my help. I just sped up the process, while pursuing my own agenda. Taking my van was an asshole move, but it really wasn't my van to begin with, it was Victor's.

The sad thing was that the possibility that she had simply stolen my vehicle and left me stranded in hostile territory was a best case scenario. If she had gone back to Dr. Klein that meant—what? Did she decide that she was better off with the devil she knew? Was the whole thing a set up? I was sure that her hate for Dr. Klein was real, and her desire to help me. If I couldn't believe that, what could I believe?

My body suddenly spun around and I saw the Quality Electrical van pulling around the corner. Godiva was driving and the back looked empty. I felt Catskinner tense.

Don't kill her—let her talk first. There could be a perfectly reasonable explanation.

perhaps. He didn't seem convinced.

When the van got close Catskinner leaped, snatched the door open and swung inside in one smooth motion. Godiva flinched back and the van jerked across the oncoming lane. Luckily no one was coming.

Catskinner directed his attention to the back. No one was there. Nothing seemed out of place.

"I had to leave," Godiva said in a rush, looking panicked. "Cops, they were driving real slow, like they were looking for someone. I ducked down when I saw them, but I was scared they were going to come back. I've been driving around the block."

"did they go to dr. klein's house?"

"I think so. They were headed that way."

"drive to the highway."

Godiva nodded and made a turn at the next intersection. She kept glancing over at me warily, like she was expecting Catskinner to hit her.

perfectly reasonable?

Close enough. Let me talk to her.

"We're going to Lindbergh and Forty," I told her.

Godiva smiled over at me, her face lighting up. "You're not mad?" she asked.

"No, I think you did the right thing."

A pause. Then, "Is *he* mad?"

"Catskinner doesn't get mad."

i get even.

You get odd, I countered.

"Did you kill her?" Godiva asked. She was looking straight ahead, her voice carefully neutral.

"No," I said. "The cops came when I was asking her questions, and I had to run." I studied her profile, but I couldn't tell how she felt about Dr. Klein still being alive. Maybe she wasn't sure herself.

"She said she was going to leave town," I added.

A nod. "She was always talking about going to Paris. She went to school there for a couple of years, she always wanted to go back."

"You ever hear of a place called The Good Earth?"

"Sure, Dr. Klein bought stuff from there all the time. Is that where we're going?"

"That's where I'm going. How about Keith Morgan?"

She chewed her lip. It was a cute gesture. "She used to talk to a guy named Keith. I thought maybe he was her boyfriend and he was married."

Interesting. "What makes you say that?"

"She was always kind of paranoid about his calls. Kept her voice real low. Like she didn't want anyone to hear."

We got back on the main street and I realized I was starving. "Hang on, let's stop for food first."

"Sure. And, uh, can you drive? I don't have a license."

Now she tells me. "Pull into Subway."

I got myself a footlong. Godiva claimed she wasn't hungry. I wondered if she just didn't want to give me another opportunity to see her eat. I hadn't looked before, or at least I'd tried not to, but it was clear that she didn't eat the same way that normal people eat. Of course, neither did I, since I had to deal with my body being hijacked by Catskinner on a regular basis. It could be that she really wasn't hungry, I wasn't good at judging a reasonable food intake.

While I was eating I asked her about the blue metal boys and the nova crew. She'd overheard Dr. Klein mention both of them, but didn't know who they were. She had a little more information about the nests.

"I think it's some kind of cult. There were a bunch of guys who came over to do work around the place, building the booths and moving stuff. They looked like they were brainwashed or something, they all looked the same and they didn't talk. Creepy."

About six hundred calories later I was pulling onto the highway. We drove in silence for a while and then I turned on the radio. I wasn't any good at small talk.

As I drove I kept glancing at her. She was singing silently along with the radio, her soft lips moving gently to the rhythm. She didn't seem to be looking at me, but I couldn't tell where those strange eyes were focused behind her sunglasses. I didn't quite know what to think of her. Her body in the seat beside me was like a pin-up made flesh, all curves and warmth and soft smooth skin. I remembered how it felt to hold that body close against mine. I wanted that, I wanted her close beside me, but I knew the danger of wanting.

I found myself thinking about her strangeness—her green-in-green eyes, her toothless mouth, the way her jaw moved. I wondered how deep that strangeness went, what more was covered by her clothes.

I remembered what she'd said, what she'd promised in exchange for food. I'd gotten her food and part of me wanted to take her up on it. Just once, a body like that, under me, doing what I wanted—

She was looking at me, then, and my eyes met her sunglasses. She smiled, wide and open, as if she knew just what I was thinking and liked it.

Dangerous. Very dangerous.

I took a deep breath, let it out. Time to come back to reality.

"Where do you want me to drop you off?" I asked.

She looked sharply over at me. "I'm going with you."

I shook my head. "You can't."

"I can't?" Her eyebrows peeked over the top of her sunglasses.

"You can't," I repeated. "In the first place, I don't know where I'm going. And in the second place... I'm not a good person. You don't want to go anywhere with me."

"I think I do," she said softly.

That made me angry. Soft things, nice things, they weren't part of my life. Never had been, never could be. "Well, you're wrong. Look, this thing inside me, it kills people. It's very, very good at it."

"But it's not you."

"Yes! Yes, it is." I tried to calm myself. "Catskinner and me, we're part of the same thing. I am a monster." Surely I could make her understand that.

"You're not the only one."

That gave me pause. I looked over at her for a moment, then back at the road. She wasn't human, or not entirely human, I reminded myself.

"This is not going to have a happy ending." I tried again, "People are going to get hurt. People are going to die. Maybe you."

A dry chuckle. "I'm hard to kill."

Well, that was something we had in common.

"I don't—" I began.

"I do," she interrupted me.

"You do what?"

"You were going to say that you don't know where you're going or what you're doing. I do. I'm going with you, and I'm going to do whatever you're doing. The only way you're going to stop me is to throw me out of the van, and I don't think you're going to do that."

Before I could answer Catskinner did. *"he wouldn't. i would."*

A slow nod. "Yes, you would. You'll kill me if you think I'm a threat to you."

"yes."

"I'm not. I can help you. I know things that you don't know. Things that you need to know."

Catskinner didn't answer her. After a while I did, slowly, stumbling over the words. "Do you know what you're asking me? If Catskinner decides you're dangerous, he'll kill you. He'll use my body to do it and I won't be able to stop him. Do you understand that? I'll have to watch you die."

"Is he really that much stronger than you are?"

I shrugged. "Yes. No. I don't know. Strength really isn't the issue. It's . . . he's so fast. When he acts, I usually don't even know what he's doing until it's over."

She chewed that over. "I do understand, James. I won't make you watch me die."

I wished I could believe that. Inside I said, she's no threat to us. Honestly.

you want her with us.

I do.

it is a mistake.

Maybe. But she really does have useful information.

No answer, at least no answer in words. Instead I felt his focus, shift, relax a bit. It was if Catskinner was no longer painting a target on her forehead—that's the best way I can explain it.

I relaxed, too.

"I'm not going to throw you out of the van," I said.

She smiled at me. "I like you," she said. "It's like Stockholm syndrome."

"What?" It wasn't the most flattering thing anyone had ever said to me.

"It's when a hostage falls in love with her captor," Godiva explained.

"I know what it is," I groused. "You're not a hostage. I tried to get rid of you, remember?"

She looked up at me, her sunglasses reflecting my face back at me. "What am I?"

a mistake.

Catskinner's tone was amused. Aloud I said, "You're the princess."

She smiled at that, and her tongue flickered over her lips. "And you're the knight who rescued me." She leaned up against me. Catskinner didn't react at all.

"No, I'm the dragon," I corrected her.

She chuckled. "Silly. The dragon doesn't rescue the princess."

"I never was any good at playing by the rules."

She moved in her seat and we were no longer in contact, but I was intensely aware of her closeness.

"We should get cell phones," she said suddenly. "So I can call you if I have to move the van or anything. So we won't get separated."

I nodded, just to be agreeable. I'd never had a cell phone. I'd never had anyone I wanted to keep in contact with before Victor, and he never left his office. Thinking about cell phones made me think about the future. I'd never been good at that. Life had always been to simple for plans—I was the monster and the world was filled with villagers with pitchforks and torches, and all I had to do was stay away from them. Victor had shown me that I wasn't the only monster in the world, but working with Victor had been close enough to working alone that I scarcely noticed any difference.

Godiva felt different. I didn't know why. I had known her less than two hours. I didn't really know anything about her except that we were both caught up in something that neither of us understood.

I didn't even know if we were on the same side, or how many sides there were, or what any of them were trying to accomplish.

Screw that. Life was simple. Catskinner and me, we were one side. Everybody else, the other side. And as far as I was concerned, they were outnumbered.

The Good Earth was a freestanding building that looked like it used to be a fast food restaurant. Half the lot—the half that included the drive-thru window—was fenced off. Inside the fenced area was a collection of lawn decorations—concrete fountains, statues of nymphs and gnomes, trees in pots. The other half of the lot had only one vehicle, a battered white pickup with a camper shell. If that was Keith Morgan's truck then there shouldn't be any customers. Good, we could get right down to business.

I parked the van and Godiva next door, at a convenience store.

"What are you going to do?" she asked me.

"Ask him some questions. After that . . . I dunno. Play it by ear."

"Be careful." She looked serious.

Catskinner smiled back at her. *"i won't let anything bad happen to james. keeping him safe is my job."*

And then we were across the empty parking lot and at the door. Catskinner put my hand on the door, but I opened it.

Chapter Seven

"there is always more that isn't than that which is."

The space was big and cluttered. The internal walls and partitions had been torn out and shelves put in, big industrial shelving units, some metal, some plastic, none of them matching. On the shelves merchandise was strewn, in no evident pattern.

Directly in front of me was a display of aquarium supplies, chemicals, fish food, bags of that weird colored gravel. A plastic mermaid sat at eye-level, faced turned towards a ceramic figure of a diver in an old fashioned brass helmet.

To my left was a dead end, a pallet stacked with bags of fertilizer. So I turned right. There were shelves of vitamins and supplements and such, in bright colors with words like organic and healthy all over them. Then the aisle turned right again. The store wasn't laid out like a regular store, the shelves were butted together, making a single path that wound along side the front windows—charcoal briquettes and lighter fluid to my left—then turned again, to the right again.

I still hadn't seen anyone, but my eye caught movement in the center of the store, behind the shelves.

"Hello?" I ventured.

"Good afternoon," a voice called back. Cheerful and male.

I went around the next corner and saw more of the same: a single aisle stretching around the side wall leading to yet another right turn. The place was a spiral, I realized. Shopping for obsessives.

I kept going.

Do spirals mean anything to you?

difficult places to get out of.

Yeah, they meant that to me, too.

I made two more right turns, winding my way to the center of the shop. Along the way I passed shelves of plant cuttings, a display of what seemed to be air tanks, bags of pea gravel, more vitamins—these labeled in some Asian language—a rack of knives. If there was any method to the inventory I couldn't see it.

"Looking for something?" the cheerful voice asked.

"Just . . . looking." I could see glimpses of the man in the middle. He looked short and fat and blond, that was about all I could tell.

Right turn, right turn, past bug spray and T-shirts and hard candy, dried fish in crinkly plastic bags, right turn past a pallet loaded with bolts of cloth that looked like silk, and I was in the center of the spiral.

The counter in the center of the store was more normal looking than I expected. A big box with a Formica top and a cash register and a display of lighters with skulls and flags on them, and behind all that a short pudgy guy with long blond hair and goatee wearing a Star Wars T-shirt. He smiled at me.

"Welcome."

"Are you Keith Morgan?"

"I am. And you're James Ozwryck."

"Then you know why I'm here."

"I could guess, but I'd rather you told me."

"Why did you kill Victor and try to kill me?"

"I didn't do either one. I wasn't even there. I'm sure Madeline told you that much."

"You gave her the Seal of Solomon. That almost killed me."

He frowned, nodded. "That was a bad move on her part. But, honestly, what would you have done if she released you?"

Catskinner answered for me. "*torn her apart.*"

He nodded again. "See? There really wasn't a good move for that situation. By leaving you she gave you a chance. Obviously, it worked."

"Why Victor?"

He sighed. "Do you mind if I smoke?"

"Sure, go ahead."

Catskinner's attention was focused on Morgan's hands like a laser, but he just shook a cigarette out of a pack and lit it with one of the lighters from the display. Clove, by the smell.

"Okay," he let out a cloud of sweet smoke. "You know Victor was undead, right?"

Undead? I suppose that word fit what I knew of his condition, but it seemed overly theatrical. I shook my head.

"I know he was my friend."

"I know he's a vampire, but he's still my brother!" Said with a grin.

"He never drank blood. Whatever he was, he wasn't a vampire."

"Sorry." Keith waved a hand. "Lost Boys reference. I'm guessing pop culture isn't your strong suit."

"I want to know why we were attacked."

He took a long drag on his cigarette and let out his answer with the smoke. "I know, and I'm getting there, but I'm not sure how much I have to explain. I assume you know about the Macrobes?"

"No."

"Eldila? Outsiders? I'm not sure what you call that passenger inside you—"

"Catskinner."

He smiled at that. "Very appropriate. Well, it is what I call a 'Macrobe', a form of life that does not require a physical form. Such things are not bound by laws of physics that apply to physical objects. They exist as information, as permutations in the patterns of matter, but not actually material. You see?"

Is this true?

it's as true as that one can understand.

I nodded.

He smiled. "Good. Now, the relationship that you and . . . Catskinner have is rare. Almost unique. Most Macrobe/human interaction is more symbolic. Macrobes communicate by inspiration, visions, dreams. As I said, they are information. Information is to them what flesh and blood is to us."

"Victor." I prompted.

"Relax, I'm getting there. There is an entire Macrobial ecology. There are big ones, little ones, predators, prey—just like the biological ecology we have on Earth. Many Macrobes have an interest in terrestrial matters—they find physical life just as fascinating as we find immaterial life. They communicate with humans, some humans, those that they find . . . interesting. They make deals."

He was warming to his subject, talking with his hands. He talked like he was explaining a new religion to a possible convert.

I wasn't impressed. "When do we get to the part where you tell me why I shouldn't kill you?"

"Soon," he promised, holding up a hand. "Victor was in communication with a particular Macrobe, one that passed on to him certain information, technology, if you will. That's how he was able to maintain an anathanotic homeostasis—how he became undead."

"And Dr. Klein?"

"Is in communication another one. One from a competing . . . tribe, you might say. Two alien intelligences at war, using human pawns to do their fighting in the physical realm. Essentially, you got caught in the crossfire. Since your . . . tenant is not allied with either side, the decision was made to neutralize you, but not kill you. You do realize that Dr. Klein could have simply cut your throat while you were paralyzed."

"I still don't have an answer to my question."

"Why you shouldn't kill me? There are a number of reasons." He ticked them off on his fingers, "First, I'm no threat to you. I function as an intermediary between the Macrobes' human envoys. I am, myself, not directly aligned with any celestial faction. Secondly, I would be dangerous for you to kill, for the same reason. I am valuable to many very powerful creatures. As you've observed, continual communication with these intelligences has a teratogenic effect on human beings. They change, and those changes can make it difficult for them to interact with the mass of humanity. I do a fair amount of legwork for things much more dangerous than you. Thirdly, I can be useful to you—we can be useful to each other. I am well aware of your unique abilities. I can put you in touch with those who would pay handsomely."

He smiled and curled his outstretched fingers into a fist. "Lastly, you might find that I am not as easy to kill as you suppose. The Macrobes pay their employees in strange coin."

I nodded. What he said made sense. Something didn't add up, though. "Dr. Klein said that you paid her to kill Victor and destroy his book."

"Did she now?" for a moment his affable manner dropped and his eyes were cold. Then the smile came back. "I suppose she was trying to deflect your ire from herself. I assure you, she approached me for the Seal, and she paid me for it. I had no reason to attack Victor or you."

"And she paid you to arrange the workers from the Manchester nest?"

A slow nod. "Yes, she did." He smile was starting to look forced. "As I said, I'm a middleman. A broker, if you will."

What do you think?

he probably is too dangerous to kill.

Did you know about other Macrobes working with humans?

i know that there are thrones and dominions in the vasty deep and the wars of heaven are mirrored and shadowed in this tide pool. as above, so below, as ever was.

Were you planning to mention this to me?

were you planning on telling me that you didn't know?

I shook my head. Infuriating as always.

Keith was watching me warily.

"Suppose," I said at last, "that I did want you to broker my services. How would that work?"

The smile was back, wider than ever. "Take a walk with me," he suggested. He came out from behind the counter and began walking the spiral path to the door.

"I'm surprised the fire department lets you operate with this setup," I said, falling in behind him.

A laugh. "They don't know I exist. This is a hard place to find if I don't want it to be found."

"One of those strange coins?"

He glanced back at me. "Exactly so."

He walked briskly passed the random merchandise.

"Dr. Klein mentioned blue metal boys and the nova crew. I guess those are other Macrobe factions?"

He didn't look back at me. His voice was cold. "You certainly caught Madeline in a garrulous mood."

Catskinner answered through my mouth. *"i induced a garrulous mood."*

That earned a look back. "I expect you did. Is she still alive, by the way?"

"She was when I left her."

That seemed to satisfy him. "Yes, I do business with a half dozen Macrobe envoys. There, perhaps, fifteen or twenty operating on Earth at the moment. Some don't operate in this area, some are . . . insular, and some I refuse to work with." We stopped before we reached the front door, and I noticed a small side door between two displays that I hadn't seen on the way in. Keith pulled a key ring from his pocket and unlocked it. "Believe me, your Catskinner isn't the worst entity on this planet, not by a long shot."

He pushed the door open. It led to the fenced part of the lot. I followed him out into his strange garden. The fenced area outside was just as cluttered as the shop had been. Lawn furniture, concrete fountains, statues, all of it scattered around in no obvious pattern. There were aisles between the merchandise out here, curving at seeming random through the kitsch.

Keith lit another clove cigarette and sat down on a green painted Adirondack chair. He waved me to the bench opposite him. It seemed solid enough, so I sat down. Beside us a fountain in the shape of a leaping fish dribbled water into a bowl held by a nymph.

"Okay," he began, "the first thing you have to realize is that Macrobes don't deal in money—not directly. They deal in knowledge, knowledge is power, money is power, so the rewards are there. They just take a little work sometimes to monetize."

I nodded.

"They have means of perception that are beyond human comprehension. They can . . . see things that we can't. They know things that we don't, and that's what they trade. Let me give you an example: suppose that one entity wants another entity's human operatives taken out. Killed. It can't just give you a briefcase full of hundred dollar bills. What it could do, however, is tell you the location of a rich vein of gold. They can sense things like that, isolate individual elements through the rock.

"But," he continued, "we still have to do the work of buying the land, getting a mining company to do the tests to see the gold is there, get the permits to dig, all that. You see?"

"I understand."

He smiled and puffed on his cigarette. "So I'll tell you this up front—I take a big cut. I've got my fingers in a lot of different industries, I've got a lot of contacts. People—certain select people— trust me. It takes a lot of overhead to maintain these contacts."

"How big a cut?" I was beginning to really dislike this man, but I wanted to keep him talking.

"Depends on the contract." He shrugged, stubbed out his cigarette and lit another. The smell of cloves was something else I was really starting to dislike. "I mean, how do you figure the return on something like a new invention? Long term, short term, points after development costs? But, the thing is, I take care of my people. If it's money you're after, trust me, you'll have more than you can ever spend."

He leaned forward and looked me straight in the eye. "I can offer you a million in cash as a retainer. A signing bonus. I can have it in your hands by tomorrow morning."

I believed him. If he was profiting from alien technology, a million was nothing. I looked around the fenced lot, the scattered statues and fountains and lawn chairs.

He grinned. "I don't need to impress anybody. I could have a skyscraper in downtown Manhattan with my name on it, but who wants that kind of attention? Real power doesn't have to advertise."

I thought about it. Did I want a million dollars? I thought about being rich, having a big house, big cars, fancy clothes, expensive electronic toys.

My parents had been rich.

"And money is just the tip of the iceberg. The icing on the cake." Once again he seemed to know what direction my thoughts were taking. "I won't say that you have no idea what the Macrobes can do—obviously you're familiar with the advantages that your tenant can bestow upon you—but there is so much more. The technology they can share with us. Medicine, computers, materials—centuries, who knows? in advance of anything we can do. The sky's the limit, and I mean that literally."

A thought occurred to me. Has this human been altered?

yes. the threads of existence have been double-woven.

Which does what?

death will not come swift to this one.

"So what happens now? Do I just leave you my number and you'll call me when something comes up?"

A smile, a nod, and another cigarette. "Basically, yes. There is the matter of reaching an accord with your tenant, of course."

That was just a little too casual. "Accord?"

An airy wave of his hand. "It's customary when dealing with Macrobes to have a covenant to protect both parties."

"no." Catskinner's voice surprised me.

"Hear me out. I'm not talking about a binding, simply a covenant. The terms will simply be—"

"i'll not write nor speak any oath upon you, conjure man."

Catskinner had taken my body while he spoke. He stood and faced Keith.

Keith sighed. "Choose your words with care, child of the morning star."

"the word i choose is no. no terms. no conditions. no covenant."

What is he asking for that you won't do?

a slave collar.

Okay, let's go. I thought this deal sounded too good to be true.

"I urge you to reconsider," Keith said softly. It sounded like a threat.

"these negotiations are concluded." Catskinner turned to head back to the store.

"I had really hoped that we could do business." Keith dropped his clove cigarette into the water of the fountain beside him.

And the water came alive.

Chapter Eight

"if it bleeds, it can die, but not everything bleeds."

At first it looked like just a big splash, as if the cigarette butt had been a brick. Then the tendrils of water elongated impossibly and whipped towards my head. Catskinner was already moving, spinning and dropping out of their path. I remember thinking, what's the big deal, it's only water, when I saw one of the tendrils slice through a concrete statue of a satyr, decapitating it without slowing.

Dimly I was aware of Keith walking away, heading deeper into the maze of concrete and cheap painted wood, but my point of view was in violent motion as Catskinner dodged the animated water.

What is that?

airish beast by diverse numbers deceived.

It looked more waterish than airish to me, but I figured it wasn't a good time to insist on a complete explanation.

Can you kill it?

it is not alive.

Which probably meant no. I shut up—I didn't want to distract him.

He lashed out at the bench where Keith had been sitting and it was splinters and the splinters were in my hand and then—thoop!, thoop!, thoop!—they were severing a handful of the liquid tendrils. The water that was separated from the main body fell to splash on the asphalt, but more rose out of the nymphs bowl and scythed, glittering in the sunlight like fishing line coated with diamond dust towards me and I wasn't there. My perspective was spinning wildly out of control. If I'd had control of my stomach I would have been sick, but my body was cool and distant, something I had owned once but had no particular interest in now.

More water was in motion than that bowl could have held. I wondered where it came from. I wondered how it was moving, what force animated it against all the laws of physics I knew about. I wondered if it would kill me and how it would feel to die. I couldn't feel real fear—Catskinner had an iron grasp on my endocrine system as well as the rest of my flesh—but I very much did not want to die.

Metal whistled through the air, thrown by a hand I recognized as mine, and the nymph statue disappeared in an explosion of shattered concrete. The bowl clattered onto the ground and then hell really and truly broke out.

Water surged upward into a tower, vaguely man-sized with tendrils spinning off in all directions. Catskinner dove past gnome-dryad-deer-windmill-love seat-mailbox and a rain of splintered lawn ornaments followed, blood from punctures visible on the parts of my skin I could see.

i can't calve off enough matter to break the sequence, which might not have been directed at me, since I didn't understand it, and both of my hands were busy, hurling bits of metal and rock at the tendrils, cutting them loose to splash on the ground. The main mass withdrew the tendrils it had remaining and began oozing towards me, leaving a glistening trail behind it. It seemed to be gaining mass as it went. Maybe it was condensing water out of the air. Catskinner kept peppering it with whatever came within reach of my hands, but the splashes weren't making it lose enough water to make any difference.

Maybe if you kill Keith? I suggested.

that would not unravel the construct.

How about running away?

The mass of water started extruding tentacles, big ones this time. They flailed slower than the little tendrils had, but struck with enough force to smash through the furniture in its path. Catskinner seemed to agree with me about running away. He was heading towards the wrought iron fence.

The water thing was heading to cut us off, and it could smash through things that Catskinner had to move over or around. I caught something out of the corner of my eye.

See if you can lead it to the right, I suggested. Catskinner obligingly jumped that way, flipped over the top bar of a swing set and landed next to what I'd seen—a pallet load of bags.

Stand on that, I said, and he did. The water thing oozed towards us, trashing the swing set on the way. Now run for the fence—

The water thing struck the pallet moments after Catskinner left it. As I'd hoped, it hit the bags hard enough to burst them open, and clouds of sand flew everywhere. Dry sand.

I didn't see what the sand did to the water thing because Catskinner was sprinting for the fence. I hoped that it had killed it or deactivated it or whatever, but all it had to do was slow it down for a few seconds. The space next to the fence was empty, asphalt with meandering lines of weeds growing up through the cracks.

When he was about five feet from the fence my body sprung from a crouch to a leap, aiming for the top crossbar—

—and missed the fence. The leap was perfect, arms extended, my hands already curled to grab the bar and the fence refused to get any closer. Catskinner landed and rolled, still about five feet from it. The asphalt in front of the fence was clear, leaving a kind of walkway around the lot. He sprinted towards it. I could feel my legs moving in the right direction, but we were moving parallel to the fence, not towards it. Catskinner stopped. He seemed to be as confused as I was. We were doing the running part just fine, but the away part wasn't happening.

My head looked back. The pie of wet sand was squirming, the water struggling to dump the weight of the sand. It didn't look like it was down for the count or even for very long.

Catskinner dove, rolled, jumped, and my body must have covered a good forty feet. The fence stayed five feet away.

The water construct crashed through a collection of bird feeders and Catskinner kept running, along side the fence. It maintained its maddening distance. Space was somehow warped or twisted or tied up in knots, and it wasn't going to let us out that way. We'd have to get out of here the way we came in, through the shop.

Unfortunately the water thing was that way. Even more unfortunately, so was Keith, and I had a feeling he had more tricks up his sleeve.

I caught a glimpse of him in the distance, standing by the door to the shop, arms folded. Waiting for his construct to kill me. He looked very patient. Catskinner looked the other way. I could see through the fence to the convenience store next door. My van was parked outside it. I wondered if Godiva could see me, if she could tell what was happening. I hoped that she would take the van, take the money, and escape. She deserved the chance to make a better life, away from this craziness.

As I watched my van started moving, but then I lost sight of it as Catskinner ducked and leaped over the top of the construct and back the way we'd come. The edge of the fence circled back to the shop building and whatever space warp kept us from reaching the fence didn't stop the store from getting closer. I heard a motor revving up and—

—suddenly a section of the fence slammed down next to me and my van crashed through it. Evidently the space warp trick didn't work from the outside in. Catskinner reacted and I was rolling under the van and then standing on the other side. I yanked the passenger door open.

Godiva wasn't driving.

"best to leave quickly" Catskinner said, and the driver threw the van in reverse, screeching over chunks of busted fence. Either the van hadn't gotten far enough in to get caught in the space warp, or breaking down the fence had messed up whatever was causing it. The driver was a woman, and vaguely familiar, but Catskinner wouldn't focus my eyes on her long enough for me to be sure.

The water thing was surging through the broken fence. I was kind of hoping that it couldn't cross the borders of Morgan's domain, but it had no problem coming through the gap.

Movement caught Catskinner's eye and he turned my head. The door to the store opened and Godiva came out at a run, grocery bags in her arms. She headed right for the water thing.

Stop her! I screamed in my head. Before I could even try to take my body back, Godiva threw something at the water monster, something small and green. A tendril of water sliced the object open and green stuff sprayed all around.

The construct collapsed, just like that. It sank down into a puddle of water. Whatever that stuff was, I wanted some.

The driver slowed my van and Godiva opened the sliding door and jumped into the back.

I reached to take my body back and Catskinner retreated.

careful.

I felt like hell. The hunger was bad this time and the cuts and abrasions all over my body stung. Still, I made myself sit up and look at the driver.

"I bet you're not really a leasing agent," I told her.

She was driving, pulling fast on to Lindbergh, going north. Without taking her eyes off the road she said, "I'm not. And my name's not Debbie Sawyer. It's Alice Mason."

"So what are you?"

"I'm saving your life is what I am."

I sighed. "And you just happened to be in the neighborhood?"

"No. I was following you." Well, at least she was honest.

Godiva leaned forward from the back and passed me one of the plastic bags from the convenience store. "I figured you might be hungry."

Beef jerky and chocolate. I tore into it. Between bites I asked her, "Do you know her?"

Godiva shook her head. "She just came up to the van and said you needed help."

"She was right. So what did you dump on the water monster?"

"Dish soap."

Dish soap, huh? I'd remember that.

"These kinds of constructs operate by manipulating the surface tension of the water. The soap breaks the tension so it can't keep cohesion. As soon as I saw what Morgan threw at you, I picked up a bottle," Godiva explained. We were cruising north.

"You know a lot about this stuff," I said.

Godiva shrugged. "Dr. Klein used the same kind of thing."

I looked over at Alice. "So what's your angle? And where are we going?"

"My angle is that I'm trying to save the human race."

Yeah, she would be. "Repelling the invasion of the Macrobes, huh?"

"The invasion already happened. The Earth has been occupied for centuries. I'm the resistance."

"You and who else?"

"I have investors."

Investors? "So, people pay you to save the world, then?"

"Actually people usually pay me to save one person that they care about. The world is too big for most people to love."

I chewed that over. Godiva spoke from the back. "I think we should help her."

"Hang on," I said. "I'm one of the bad guys, remember? I've got a Macrobe living in my head. And you—you've been altered by Macrobe technology."

Is Alice human? I asked Catskinner.

unaltered.

"So where are we going, anyway?" I asked. I was getting tired of not getting straight answers. From anyone.

"We're here." Alice said. We had pulled into the parking lot of a bowling alley. It was pretty full and I realized that it was Saturday evening. It seemed like a lot had happened since Friday.

"So, is the secret headquarters of the human resistance?"

Alice turned to look at me for the first time. "No, James, it's a bowling alley. It's a good place to talk without being overheard." She got out of the van, and Godiva opened her door.

"The van's a good place to talk without being overheard," I pointed out.

Godiva flashed me a grin. "Yeah, but they've got beer here."

It was hard to argue with that kind of logic.

Chapter Nine

"what is done may not always be undone."

I got out of the van. It wasn't hard to catch up to Alice. I held out my hand. "My keys?"

She handed them over.

"Thanks for coming to get me back there." It seemed like the thing to say.

Alice sighed. "You're in way over your head. We can help each other."

I chewed my lip. "Maybe."

"What I don't get," she said slowly, "is how somebody could know enough to bind an Eldil without knowing more than you seem to."

"I didn't bind it," I pointed out. "My parents did."

Her stride faltered. "Your parents? When?"

I shrugged. "I don't know. Young enough that I don't remember ever not being like this."

She stopped dead at that. "Wait a second. Where were you born?"

I hesitated, but couldn't think of any reason not to tell her the truth. "California. L. A. County."

"You're Adam Chase!"

No one had called me that for twenty years. "How do you know that name?" I could feel Catskinner focus his attention on her.

Godiva almost bumped into me. "You said your name is James," she accused.

I turned to her. "Did your folks name you Godiva?" I asked.

She looked away. "No," she said in a very small voice. Her reaction seemed strange, but I was more concerned with Alice.

"What do you know about Adam Chase?" I demanded.

Alice was walking again. "Let's get inside before we say anything else."

There were a couple of people in the parking lot, mostly coming in, a few going out. None of them seemed to be looking or listening to us, but after the day I'd had I figured paranoia was the better part of valor.

We got three beers and a table against the wall, amid the echoes of clattering pins.

"Adam Chase," Alice said, looking at me, and shook her head. "Incredible."

"My name is James Ozwryck." I told her firmly.

Godiva was looking from me to Alice.

Alice rested her chin on her hand. "Okay, James, you asked me what I know about Adam Chase. He was born in '74 or '75, as I recall. His father was Michael Chase, his mother was Sabrina Erikovitch. The two of them were the leaders of a group called Clear Vision World. They wrote a couple of books together. *We Pass From View* was one, and, uh, *The Eternal Odyssey.* I can't remember any of the other titles, but I've probably got them back in my library."

The second book was actually called *Mankind's Eternal Odyssey.* I nodded for her to continue.

"The Clear Vision World was a fairly straightforward millennial/spiritualist cult. The leaders were in contact with spirit guides from the great beyond who prophesied a coming apocalypse and that a chosen few would be spared to repopulate the new Eden—Michael Chase getting a jump on the repopulation business as usual, aside from Adam he may have had as many as ten other children. The chosen few, of course, being those who heard and believed the guidance of the spirits, because the rest of the world was too wicked, waging war, despoiling the environment, oppressing women and minorities, blah, blah, blah. Very 70s." She sounded like a lecturer or a schoolteacher.

I nodded again. None of this was news to me, except the bit about Michael Chase's other children, and that didn't surprise me.

"The only child Michael Chase ever officially acknowledged was born to Sabrina Erikovitch. A son. He was going to be the first of the new race of perfect humanity and so in a fit of originality Chase named him Adam."

She stopped and drained her beer. I did likewise. Godiva sipped hers.

"Michael did something to Adam. There really were spirits that he was in communication with, but the communication was flawed. Human minds aren't designed to accept the perspective of an alien intelligence. Too much exposure damages them. The spirits, outsiders, Macrobes—call them what you will—could influence human thought. They could send dreams and visions clearly enough teach humans new technology. They could even possess human beings, take over their bodies for a brief time, but it was like trying to send high voltage through speaker wire. The human minds would burn out over time, and the closer the connection, the faster they burned."

I glanced over at Godiva. She was listening very gravely.

"The spirits gave Michael Chase an idea, though," Alice continued. "An infant's mind is unformed, malleable. By linking together a Macrobe with a human infant, binding them, Michael hoped to create a new kind of human. The voices he heard promised that he would be the father of a new species, human bodies with alien minds, who would inherent the Earth."

Catskinner's laugh bubbled out of my mouth. *"but it didn't work out that way, did it?"*

Godiva straightened in her chair, backing away from Catskinner's voice. "What happened?"

Alice looked over at me. I could see her registering Catskinner behind my eyes.

"yes, tell us what happened to michael chase."

"He was killed in killed in April of 1982. He, Sabrina, and seven other members of Clear Vision World. The only survivor was Adam, who was seven at the time. Of course, the authorities didn't believe that a child could have murdered nine adults, so Adam was placed in an institution. A month later, he escaped, leaving six dead staff members behind him. No one has seen him since."

I had my body back. "No," I said softly, "no one has."

I got up. "You two can make your own way home." I turned to go.

"Wait," said Alice.

I kept going.

"James, please," Godiva said. That made me pause. "Just listen to her."

I sat back down. I peeled off a couple of twenties and gave them to Godiva.

"Get us some more beer. And some nachos or pizza or something, okay?"

She nodded, then smiled. She was heartbreakingly pretty. I watched her walk away, admiring the bounce in her step, and turned back to Alice.

"So, talk."

"There's a war going on, James—" she began.

"Between the humans and the Macrobes, I know." I'd picked up that much.

"No!" She leaned forward, her voice quiet but forceful. "The war is between the outsiders. Most humans have no idea that it's even happening. The outsiders don't care about humans at all—this is just a convenient place to fight. We're not even their foot soldiers, we're their ammunition."

She leaned back again. "Do you think that the spirit guide who told Michael Chase how to bind Adam cared what happened to Clear Vision World? It didn't tell him what Adam would be capable of. Those things find people who are easily led and already half crazy, and then they spin whatever lies will get things done. They claim to be angels, aliens, spirits, demons, ghosts of dead relatives, whatever they think people will listen to and obey. They do a few tricks, things they know will impress the natives, and send their pets out to fight each other. When their pet humans die, they just go out and get more. We don't even know what they are."

Her voice was getting strident, she made a deliberate effort to bring it back under control. "Do you understand that? They have been influencing human history for thousands of years, starting wars, building empires, inspiring all manner of atrocities for their own purposes, and we don't even know for certain what the fucking things are!"

"Keith Morgan called them Macrobes," I said.

She shook her head angrily. "Some science fiction writer made up that word. Morgan is as bad as they are. The crazy ones I can almost feel sorry for, but a man like Morgan who sells his soul with his eyes wide open. . . ."

She paused and Godiva came back to the table, carrying a tray with beer and pizza on it. I had expected her to take longer.

I took a beer, took a long swallow.

"What has all this got to do with me?" I asked.

Alice sighed. "Well, I could say it's because you're a human being."

"Part of me is," I corrected her.

"All of James is human."

I considered that. Nodded. Catskinner was quiet, but I could feel him listening.

"More importantly, though, all of you is in danger."

"I've got a good track record of taking care of myself."

"Against humans, sure," Alice took a sip of her beer. "But what would you have done if I hadn't broken the barrier effect when I did? You don't know what you're facing. You've kept a low profile for twenty years, you've been lucky. Or maybe the outsiders just didn't want you yet. They don't think on a human time scale, twenty years is nothing to them."

Is she telling the truth?

she is telling as much of the truth as she understands.

That was the same thing Catskinner had said about Keith Morgan.

What should we do?

avoid decay. live in shelter. survive.

Can we trust her?

"will you seek to make covenant with me?" Catskinner asked Alice.

"No. A simple agreement is all I want."

My head bobbed up and down, Catskinner trying for a nod. *"what do you ask of me?"*

A short bark of a laugh. "To start with, please don't kill me."

"if you do not seek to harm myself or james, i will not kill you."

"And listen. Listen to what I have to say and make up your own mind about where your best interests lie."

"reasonable." And he sank back out of sight. I could feel his attention, but not the hair-trigger tension I felt when he expected violence. It was more that he was simply interested in what the others had to say.

I looked over at Godiva. "Where do you fit in all this?"

She fiddled around before answering. She took a piece of pizza, put it on a plate, set it in front of her. She glanced at Alice, then looked at me, her sunglasses reflecting streaks of neon from the bar. "I was lied to," she said finally. "I don't know what to believe anymore. I thought Dr. Klein was going to help me—"her voice broke—"help me become what I wanted to be. Instead, she left me.

She just left me there, didn't even tell me she was leaving."

She picked up the pizza, threw it back down. "I can't even eat in public anymore. She made me a freak. She made me a monster."

I felt like I should say something, but Catskinner spoke first. *"be glad,"* he said, *"in this world you're either a monster or a victim."*

I gasped. I tried to find some way to unsay it. Godiva stared at me, outrage on her features, then she shook her head. "I guess you'd know."

"Yeah, I would. Story of my life." I turned back to Alice. "So what's a decent human being like you want with a couple of monsters?"

I'd intended the remark to be cutting, but if she was cut by it she gave no sign. "Mutual protection. Exchange of information." she said simply.

The pizza was cooling in front of me. I took a piece and ate it. Nobody said anything while I was eating.

Then, "Why did Dr. Klein kill Victor?" I asked.

"Keith Morgan paid her to," Alice answered. "I don't know why Morgan wanted Victor killed. It's likely he saw Victor as a threat."

"Why didn't she kill me?"

"She thought she did. A few hours stasis would have killed an ordinary servitor."

"And I'm an extraordinary servitor?"

"No, a servitor is more like a human puppet. In order to be able to use the human's body the outsider has to rebuild much of the human brain and destroy most of the existing personality. You're not like that, James. You co-exist with the outsider."

"Because we grew up together."

"Basically, yes."

"Dr. Klein said that I was just a puppet."

Alice nodded. "That's what she believed. That's been her experience."

A light went on. "The Manchester nest."

"The nests are the worst. They don't even try to maintain a facade that any human personality remains. One outsider with multiple human hosts, human bodies. Like a hive of insects."

"Ohh," Godiva breathed.

Alice looked at her sharply. "You've seen nestlings, then?"

Godiva nodded. "Dr. Klein used them to build the salon."

Alice sat back. "Interesting," she said slowly. "I didn't know that. That would have been, what, a year ago?"

Godiva shook her head. "No, not the first time. I mean when she got the place next door and rebuilt. Maybe six months ago?"

"Morgan's been dealing with the Manchester nest longer than I thought." Alice was half talking to herself. "I wonder if he deals with the others."

"Dr. Klein said that all the nests bought from him. How many are there?"

"Five that I know about," Alice said, "Did she say what they bought?"

I tried to remember. "Nettle junk, I think she said. But that might have been what she was buying."

Alice shook her head. "No, that's a hypnoteratogenic. Nests wouldn't have any use for it."

She abruptly stood. "It's late. It's been a busy day. How about we continue this at breakfast tomorrow?"

I stood. "Can I drop you off somewhere?"

"I've got a room reserved at your motel."

That was convenient. Wait a second—

"How do you know where I'm staying?"

She gave me a sideways look just short of an eyeroll. "You checked in with a credit card in your own name."

"Is it really that easy to find people like that? I thought that was just on TV."

She shrugged. "Easy? It's doable. You need to know the right people."

Godiva was standing next to me. "Can I stay with you tonight?" She was very close.

Catskinner was closer, a warm weight on my skin. "I don't think that's a good idea," I said. "I'll get you a room."

She nodded and turned away. She looked hurt and I felt for her. I felt for me, too. She was soft and warm and lovely and I very much wanted her to stay with me. I didn't know exactly what she had meant, what she offered, and I never would. Soft and warm and lovely were things that didn't happen to something like me.

I headed to the door. Alice and Godiva followed.

you want her.

Yes.

she's not human.

Neither am I.

she could be dangerous.

So am I.

When we got to the parking lot my body stopped and turned to Godiva.

"james wants you to stay with him. i do not forbid it." Beautiful. Catskinner's guide to picking up chicks.

Catskinner poured out of my face and I added, "Please."

Godiva smiled brilliantly, "I won't hurt you, I promise."

"That's not what I'm worried about."

She stepped closer and took my arm, looked up at me. Her glasses reflected my face. "I'm not afraid of you."

That was what I was worried about. She wasn't afraid of me, and she should have been.

Alice was standing nearby, looking around the parking lot like it was her idea to stand there and there was nothing awkward going on at all. I started walking again. Godiva kept a hold on my arm and fell into step with me. She twisted and then my arm was around her shoulders. She felt good there, warm, and she smelled good.

Chapter Ten

"the purpose of life is to expand. each worm intends to engulf the universe."

As I opened the door to my little motel suite I realized that I hadn't found time to do any shopping for food to stock the kitchenette. For some reason that really bothered me. I felt like I should have something to offer Godiva. Beer, pretzels, mini pizzas made from English muffins and spaghetti sauce—something. Wasn't that what people did when they invited someone into their home? I wasn't real clear on the etiquette.

"I'm sorry," I said. "I don't have much here."

She didn't seem to mind, though. She sat her shopping bag on the little round table under the hanging lamp and flopped down in one of the green vinyl and wood chairs that flanked it. She smiled and slipped off her shoes.

"So..." I wasn't sure what to say.

Godiva looked up at me expectantly.

"Alice Mason. Do you figure that's her real name?"

"Real enough." she shrugged. "It's something to call her, anyway."

I nodded. I figured names weren't really important, so long as you had something to call people other than "hey, you!" I couldn't quite put my finger on what was important, though. Loyalty? Fealty, maybe? I was used to thinking in terms of me against the world, the idea that there might be sides and that I might be on the same side as someone else was hard to wrap my head around. "Can I trust her, do you think?"

She chewed her lip. Still a cute gesture. "I think she's honest about what she wants."

"What's that?"

"She wants people free from the Outsiders. Free from their influence. She used to do some kind of anti-cult counseling. You know, deprogramming. I guess she found out some cults have real spirit voices running them."

I thought about that. Yeah, it made sense. "I can't be free of Catskinner. He's part of me. He's all I've got."

"I know." She looked down at the floor. "What I can't understand is what Catskinner wants."

I opened my mouth to say something—I'm not sure what—and I felt him speaking through me. "*continuity of existence. rationality of environment. silence.*"

"Safety?" suggested Godiva.

My body nodded. "*safety. food, water, air, integrity of circulatory system. sleep without vigilance for james. body of motion, body of light in parallel.*"

"What happens to you if James dies?" she asked softly.

"*unweaving.*"

"You die? You don't go back . . . someplace?"

"*there are no places, only patterns.*"

"You can only exist as long as James' . . . pattern is safe, then. Only as long as he's alive."

"*yes.*"

"And you'll do whatever you have to do to keep him alive."

"*yes.*"

"And what about keeping him happy?"

Silence from Catskinner. "I don't think he understands the question." I said. "Happiness isn't something he can quantify."

"He doesn't have to quantify it," Godiva scowled. "He just has to respect it."

"i respect that james requires environmental elements that i do not perceive directly. is that happiness?"

A blank look, then a chuckle from Godiva. "Yeah, I think that'll do as a working definition for now."

"then i will do what will keep james happy."

"Even if it means going against your own kind?"

"i have no kind."

"Other outsiders, I mean."

"i have no kind."

Godiva considered that. "Are you saying that you're unique. Sui generis?"

"yes."

Godiva leaned forward, looking up at my face. "Did you," she spoke slowly, considering each word, "Catskinner, did you . . . exist prior to James?"

"no."

She leaned back. "Huh. Now that's interesting."

She pulled out a napkin wrapped bundle from her shopping bag. The rest of the pizza. I hadn't seen her grab it.

As I looked at her I realized that what she had in that little bag was all she had in the world. I knew what that felt like. She was sitting there with a brave little grin and my heart went out to her.

"We'll go shopping tomorrow," I promised her. "Get you some more clothes."

She tugged on the hem of her T-shirt. "Yeah, this is kind of blah."

Then, in case she was waiting for me to say something, I said, "Go on, I won't watch."

I turned away to the little kitchenette. There were fresh glasses wrapped in plastic. I unwrapped two, filled them with cold water. I could hear her behind me, eating. I sipped water.

Along with my sympathy for her there grew an anger—no, a rage—that was as old to me as life. Someone made her into something rich and strange, something that I didn't understand and I wasn't sure that she understood. That same person left her at the mercy of a world that I knew from bitter experience was merciless.

"Do you want me to kill Dr. Klein?" I asked. It just popped out.

She didn't say anything, so I turned around, slowly. "I can still find her, probably."

She looked over at me, seriously. Our eyes, or rather my eyes and her sunglasses, met for a long moment and she said, "No. It doesn't matter."

I wanted to help her, wanted to make her feel better. Was that all I had to offer, death? Again that rage, at those who had made me a monster.

"I just—" I shrugged. "I just don't know what to do." I turned away. I had nothing to offer Godiva except a place to rest. She'd said it herself, the dragon doesn't rescue the princess.

"James?" her voice was soft. I looked back at her.

"I'm sorry."

"Sorry?" I stared at her, wondering, "Sorry for what?"

"I'm weak," she looked down, seeming to curl into herself. "I can't do, I can't be . . . what you are."

Tears waited heavy behind my eyes. "Being what I am," I said softly, "isn't a good thing."

"You saved me," her voice was breathless, high, full of emotion.

"Only by accident," I told her. "I was trying to save myself. You just got in the way. Collateral damage."

She stood then, barefoot and unarmored, clad in a thin gray T-shirt that clung to her curves and a denim skirt and her hips slid towards me with each step and it was my turn to flinch, to run from what I wanted and what she was and her eyes behind mirrored lenses pinned me, saw me for what I was and I turned away.

"Wait," she said and I stopped. I was helpless. Catskinner could have killed her in a heartbeat, and for a moment I envied his purity. In contrast, I was a mess. I couldn't do anything except watch as she came closer to me.

"What do you want?" I snapped at her.

"I just want to make you happy." Her smile was bright and innocent and pure. Nothing that had anything to do with me.

"Why?" I asked. Before she could speak Catskinner answered me.

because she wants something from you. because she wants to use you.

I couldn't know that he was wrong and so I turned away again. I didn't look at her when she answered me.

"I want a world where everyone is happy. I want to live without fear that someone stronger than me will take what I have. I can't give everyone what they need—"

Her small, slim body pressed against mine. Her face was against my side, her voice muffled, but I could hear every word.

"I can give you what you need. Right now. Tonight."

Hating myself was a habit. It scarcely even hurt anymore, it was more like scratching an itch, peeling away a scab on infected flesh. "And what do *you* need?"

A pause. She pulled back, looked up at my face. "Do you want the truth?"

"Yes."

She pulled her sunglasses off. Her strange eyes, green in green, looked up at me. I met her gaze. I could learn to read the story in those eyes, given time.

"I need you," she breathed. Coy and tempting, the voice of all that I had never had, all the women that I had never loved, and my hands moved of their own accord, not Catskinner, but me, my own hunger, up into her hair to grasp and claim and turn her face to mine and I pressed my mouth to hers and I felt the fear then, the fear of the monster within me, and her hands, so small, so soft upon mine, telling me without words that she was not afraid—

And I kissed her. Her mouth tasted like spiced rum, sugar and cinnamon and something more exotic, intoxicating. Her lips opened and her tongue brushed mine.

It was all that I have ever wanted, her body against mine, her breasts, full and loose beneath her shirt against my chest lower than I had imagined it, my hands wanting and so afraid to touch her there, her hands against mine, guiding me, taking control, and it was too much, all too much, too soon, too late, and maybe I was crying, I don't remember.

It was too big, too much, me wanting her, her offering herself to me, and somehow she knew that. Without moving away from me she let me go, let me turn away from her and into myself and her body against mine became comfortable instead of insistent. She kissed me again, and it was different, simple human warmth, still so strange to me, but not frightening, not frightening at all.

Against the skin of my neck she whispered, "I understand."

I was glad that someone did.

She held me that night, lay against me in that rented bed, asking for nothing from me but the touch of my body. She was soft and warm and alive and she occupied the space next to my skin, a place that no one had ever been in before, and something that has always been empty in me was filled.

I slept, and she slept, and Catskinner never spoke, never moved. Not that night.

Chapter Eleven

"spiderwebs are not built for comfort."

In the morning we walked together from the room to the hotel restaurant, where Alice was waiting for us, coffee steaming in her cup. She watched us walk in together, Godiva close by my side.

When Alice looked up at me—at us—I felt another emptiness that I had not realized was there being filled. I could see her seeing not just one person and one person, but two people. A couple. A pair of monsters, perhaps, but a pair. The feeling made me put my arm around Godiva's shoulders and some feeling—perhaps the same one—made Godiva lean into me, mold herself against me. Together we took seats at the table.

Alice smiled and nodded, just as Godiva and I were the most natural things in the world, and then a young waiter came by and wrote down what we wanted to eat, which in my case was nearly everything.

Busy last night? I asked Catskinner.

watching and waiting.

Once I'd ordered I couldn't think of anything to say. Catskinner could, though.

"what happens now?"

Alice seemed able to switch gears between talking to me and talking to Catskinner without a hitch. Even Victor hadn't caught on that quick.

"Since you've let Morgan know that you're not useful to him, he'll consider you a threat." Alice glanced over at Godiva. "He might still try to recruit *you*, though." Her voice was carefully neutral.

"Recruit me as what?" Godiva asked bitterly. "The same thing I was doing for Dr. Klein? I'm out of that line of work."

Catskinner was still in the driver's seat, and I didn't interfere. I wanted to know what he was thinking, too.

"what can be done to dissuade morgan?"

Alice cocked her head to the side. "Dissuade? I didn't expect euphemisms from you."

"you want him dead."

Alice met Catskinner's gaze in my eyes. "Yes."

"you want me to do it."

"Yes."

"how do you benefit from his death?"

"He considers me a threat as well."

"why haven't you killed him?"

"I can't. I'm not good at killing."

"i am."

"Yes."

"you need me."

"We can be useful to each other."

And Catskinner sunk back down into me, became a warm alert presence across my back. It felt kind of like being pulled up on stage to follow the opening act.

Godiva wasn't touching me any more. Both she and Alice were looking at me, and I still couldn't think of anything to say.

"Okay," I tried. "So that's that."

Godiva reached across and took my hand. She started to speak, but then the waiter showed up with a lot of food. We leaned back and let him cover the table with plates. It all smelled good.

After the waiter left Godiva squeezed my hand. "You're more than a just a killer," she said softly, then turned to Alice. "He is. He's not just Catskinner's driver, you know."

Alice nodded. "And you're more than Dr. Klein's whore."

Godiva looked down. Alice reached out and took her free hand. "We can do some good."

Godiva looked up, met Alice's eye. Alice reached out and took my other hand. Now we were sitting around the table holding hands, like someone was about to start praying. Alice looked me in the eye. "All of us."

And my bacon was getting cold. I retrieved both of my hands. I never went to summer camp, never learned to sing Kumbaya, and I was hungry.

I forked in some bacon and followed it with pancakes, then coffee. It felt good.

"Who's using euphemisms now?" I asked Alice once my throat was clear. "Is 'doing some good' the new code phrase for murder?"

"No." Alice said. She reached for my hand again and I dodged her, speared some more bacon. "I meant what I said, "she continued. "I think we can do some good."

Philosophy took a backseat to protein. Then, "Good for who?"

"For whom," Godiva corrected. I glanced over at her, and she ducked her head, embarrassed, and drank her orange juice.

"Okay," I agreed. "Good for whom?"

"For us, to begin with," Alice said.

I raised an eyebrow. "Us, meaning...?"

"You. Catskinner. Me. Godiva."

"And that's to begin with?"

"Who else do you care about?"

Good question.

"Okay, we can skip that part."

"Okay," Godiva spoke up. "So we kill him. How?"

Alice looked over at her. Godiva continued. "I mean, I assume the frontal approach is out? It's not like James is going to walk up to him and say, 'Hello, you killed my father, prepare to die.'"

"Actually," I pointed out, "I killed my father."

Godiva stared at me. "Uh. The point is, that we have to have a plan."

"Agreed. We can't take him at the Good Earth. God knows what else he's got there." I looked to Alice. "Where does he live?"

"At the Good Earth."

"So much for getting him on his commute. Where else does he go?"

Alice sighed. "Nowhere."

"Everybody goes someplace," I argued. "He told me he runs this trade network. He's got to go meet people, do business."

"Everybody comes to him. From what I can see, he hasn't left the Good Earth for years."

"That is going to be a problem." I went back to my pancakes.

"We have to draw him out," Godiva said.

Alice nodded. "Somehow."

"We attack something that he has to defend. Something that he can't stand to lose."

Alice nodded, thoughtful.

"Sun Tzu," Godiva explained. "*The Art of War.*"

Alice and I had finished eating. Alice asked for the check and Godiva asked for a box to take her breakfast with her.

"I'm going back to my place," Alice said. "I have my notes there. I can figure out what will draw him out. Do you want to come with me?"

"Yes," said Godiva at the same time I said, "No."

Godiva frowned at me. "We'll catch up," I told Alice. "We need to do some shopping first." It felt strange to say, "we". Strange but good.

Godiva smiled. "Yeah, we can come over later." It felt good to hear her say it, too.

There was a Mega-Super-Ultra Store a few miles down the road, one of those big boxes that sells everything from toothpaste to lawnmowers to computers. Godiva ate in the van on the way. Once we got there I grabbed a cart and went through the grocery section while Godiva went to buy new clothes.

While I was shopping I wondered about Godiva. She seemed able to eat ordinary food, she just needed to take her teeth out to do it. I wasn't sure how that worked—I'd avoided watching because it seemed to embarrass her. Would soft foods help? I wasn't going to go as far as getting baby food, but maybe she'd like pudding. Or salsa. Or—

I didn't have any idea how to shop for another human being, much less another person who wasn't entirely human. I filled my cart with stuff that I liked, plus some pudding. Maybe I should get a blender—they sold them, too. I decided not to make any assumptions—she could tell me what she needed.

Godiva met me at the checkout line. She didn't want to let me buy her clothes, but I insisted. She might need the cash she had for an emergency. Her life seemed to be composed mostly of emergencies the last few days.

The clothes she'd selected weren't expensive, a couple of T-shirts, a blouse, a few skirts, and tennis shoes.

We went by the motel first. I'd planned just to stop long enough to put the food away, but Godiva wanted to change clothes, and that meant she wanted to take a shower first.

"I'll be really quick," she promised, her green on green eyes peeking over the top of her sunglasses. How could I refuse? I messed around on-line for a while, watched some videos of cute cats.

And listened to the sound of water running in the shower. After what actually qualified as "really quick" the water shut off and I listened to a body moving around in the bathroom, toweling off, and then, "James?"

"Yes?" Yes.

"Could you hand me my clothes, please?"

I hadn't planned on opening the door any wider than needed to pass her the bag from the box store—or maybe I did, I'm not sure. But the door opened wide and she didn't stop it, and there I was holding the bag, and there she was, damp from the shower, toweling her head, naked.

Her body was lovely, and I couldn't look away. Tanned to a rich gold, smooth, voluptuous. Her hair, damp, was a darker gold. Her breasts were as full and ripe as any pin-up model, the waist below tight and slim. I knew I was staring, couldn't help myself. Her body captivated me. Her legs were muscular, curved and smooth. Between them—

Between her legs was a penis and testicles, lightly furred with golden hair.

My experiences with pin-up girls had not prepared me for that.

I was still staring, and I suppose my expression changed. Godiva's body language changed, from coquettish to alarmed. I looked back to her face, met her deep green eyes.

"Uh," I said. I handed her the bag.

"You didn't know," she said softly. She? Yes, she. It's what she wanted to be called.

"No."

"I thought Catskinner . . ."

Did he? In broad outline, I guess he did. "He's not real clear on details."

She wrapped the towel around herself. "I assumed you knew. Last night, I wouldn't have—"

"It's okay," I said. "I mean, it's okay. It, uh, looks good on you." Wow, that was awkward.

I turned away. I felt rather than saw her withdraw into herself, huddling in the towel. I couldn't leave it like that. Catskinner's the monster; I'm just along for the ride.

"Wait," I turned back to her. She looked up at me, wrapped in a towel, hair still damp, without her glasses or her teeth. She wasn't human. I had been making her human in my head, I realized, trying to keep her in a category that she didn't fit any more. Whatever had been done to her placed her outside the Earth, beyond the realm of the terrestrial. Just like me.

I took her in my arms, felt her warm body against mine. She held herself stiffly for a moment, then relaxed against me. Her eyes, green on green, grew liquid, and I realized that whatever she had become, she still could cry.

"It's okay," I said, not sure what I meant, but knowing that I meant it. Whatever it was, if it wasn't okay, well, then Catskinner and I would make it okay. Provided that it was something that could be made okay by violence. In my experience, most things could, but I'd be having some new experiences lately. Maybe a new approach was called for.

I kissed Godiva on her forehead, just above her strange eyes, and she smiled at me.

"We should get going," she said softly, and in no more than ten minutes we were. Godiva was dressed in her new clothes, teeth in, glasses on, and she was beautiful.

Alice Mason's base of operations turned out to be a four-family flat in Maplewood just off the highway. The ride there was surprisingly non-awkward. Godiva turned on the radio and sang softly along.

There was an asphalt parking lot behind the building with an ancient pickup truck partially covered by a tarp in the corner and big blue sedan next to it. I parked in the opposite corner, facing out. Just in case I needed to leave in a hurry.

Alice Mason's address ended in 1E, so I knocked on the first floor door on the east side. She answered in jeans and a T-shirt, which made her look younger and less intimidating than her suit.

She smiled to see us, which made me think that she wasn't sure we were coming. "Please, come in," she said.

She knew all about doing the guests coming over thing, got me some soda and Godiva some tomato juice (with a straw). Her office was big and full of stuff—books and papers and computers—but it looked organized. I still wasn't exactly sure what she did, but she seemed to be pretty good at it. She had some comfortable chairs and I sat down, drank some soda, and all at once I realized that I didn't have the slightest idea what to say.

Godiva and Alice were both looking at me expectantly. Me?

"So," I started, then "Well," followed by "Uhm." Catskinner, naturally, had nothing to add.

Godiva flashed me a smile and looked back to Alice. "The obvious place to start is the Manchester nest."

Alice folder her hands. "Okay," she said in that way that means "tell me more."

Godiva leaned forward. "First, there's no question of how James knew about them—he got the information from Dr. Klein. We don't want to advertise your involvement right away."

"I drove the van through Morgan's fence," Alice pointed out.

"True," Godiva conceded. "But are we sure he knows that? It was a busy couple of minutes there."

Alice nodded for Godiva to continue.

"Next, it's a sitting target. They're too big to move and too strange to hide. I mean, I know about them, and I'm nobody."

I was going to object to that, but she was still talking.

"They're well connected, which is part of being on the high profile side of low profile. This is an intelligence gathering exercise as much as anything else. Everybody knows them and they know everybody."

"Don't you think Morgan will see it as an obvious move, too?" Alice asked.

"Of course he will. But how much is he willing to invest in protecting them? Warn them we might be coming? Yeah, that doesn't cost anything. Offer them some extra gear in exchange for favors to be named later? Sure, that strengthens his position no

matter what. But he's not going to go out on a limb for them—
they're too easy to replace. Expendable."

I was confused. "So, if they are expendable, why attack them?"

Godiva smiled at me. "Well, information, like I said, and because
it is an obvious move. Every move tells your opponent something
about your overall strategy, the more obvious the move, the less
you reveal."

"We have an overall strategy?" That was news to me.

"Harass Morgan's interests until he's forced to respond by
coming out into the open where we can kill him," Godiva said.

That did sound familiar, particularly the killing him part. I
nodded.

Godiva looked back at Alice. "Now, what can you tell us about
the nest?"

It turned out to be quite a lot. She told us there were at least
sixteen nestlings, maybe as many as twenty. She had pictures of
about a dozen of them—ordinary looking people, for the most
part, in their twenties and thirties, but with a universally distant
look in their eyes, as if they were all listening to something no one
else could hear.

"Now, you say they are all . . . possessed by a single outsider.
Like a hive mind or something?"

Alice nodded. "What one knows, they all know. One creature
with thirty-two eyes and thirty-two arms."

"And it, or they, can do what Catskinner can do? That fast, that
tough?" Not good.

Alice shook her head. "The Nest doesn't have that kind of deep
connection with the host bodies. It's like the difference between
driving a car by sitting in it and using a remote control on RC toys—
in this case, a whole bunch of RC toys. They'll be coordinated, but
no one host is going to be any more than human—less in a lot of
ways."

That made sense. I nodded.

meat toys. no more than obstacles.

Yeah, I get the picture.

Alice had an architectural plan for the department store, although she cautioned us that the nest was sure to have extensively remodeled it in ways that would be impossible to predict. "Remember, it's not built for humans, it's built for the outsider that uses humans as its hands. Don't expect it to make sense."

Like any part of this plan made sense. "Look," I interjected. "I'm really not sold on this whole thing. Can't we just leave him alone and trust him to leave us alone? Why do we have to go picking a fight?"

Godiva chewed her lip. "Maybe. It's possible we can negotiate a truce, but we'll need to be able to negotiate from a position of strength, and that means we need more information than we have."

I looked to Alice. "You've got plenty of information. I mean"—I waved my hand around the office, the books and papers—"you've been studying all these groups."

She nodded slowly. "I've been studying them from the outside. All told, there's maybe a thousand people in the metro area that I have reason to believe are involved with outsiders. There could be five times as many that I don't know about—or twenty times as many. It's taken me ten years to learn what I know."

"And what's that?"

A sigh. "Mostly that I wish I didn't know as much as I do." She leaned back in her chair. "Look, you don't owe me anything, either of you. If you want to just walk away, I won't try to stop you. I think it'd be a mistake, but I won't try to stop you."

"Morgan never leaves his shop," I pointed out. "What if I leave town, go to California or Florida or someplace?"

"Morgan has contacts all over the world. He knows who you are now, and he'll sell that information. Adam Chase is a very valuable commodity in certain circles."

"a very hazardous commodity." Catskinner pointed out.

"Agreed," Alice said. "But consider that Dr. Klein was able to immobilize you. The same capabilities that make you dangerous make you valuable, and there are those who would spend a great deal of effort to find you and try to control you, or kill you. I know you want to go back to the way things were, but I don't think that's an option."

Godiva put her hand on mine. "Like it or not, you're on board, and you're an important piece. We don't know just how important, not yet. That's one of the things we have to find out. You can play your own game, or you can be part of someone else's. But you can't just resign—they'll kill you."

I chewed that over for a while.

"Okay," I said, "so what's our move?"

Chapter Twelve

"time is a machine for manufacturing endings."

Manchester road, once you get out of the city, is pretty much all strip malls and box stores. I was beginning to see how the outsiders kept their activities secret—it wasn't so much invisibility as obscurity. Human beings see what they want to see, and nobody wanted to see a vast conspiracy of extra-dimensional aliens (or whatever they are). At least, sane people didn't, and the crazy people were easy to recruit.

The address Alice gave us was behind a scrim of ragged trees shielding it from the road. I almost missed the turnoff into the parking lot. It was angled both back and down and I had to slow down to a crawl. Fortunately no one was behind me. The lot continued to slope down, and the top of the building was nearly at the level of the street.

It had been a big department store in better days. The sign across the top read "Happy Lucky Products" in faded gold letters. There was the glow of neon in the window, but aside from that, the place looked abandoned. The other signs were weathered to illegibility and the parking lot a mess of frost heave and straggly grasses. There were cars in the lot, however, a half dozen of them. Some of them could have belonged to shoppers, but I suspected that most of them belonged to the nest.

I parked away from the other cars, on the side of the building. Again I felt that sense of isolation from the human world, as if the busy street just across the lot might as well have been on the other side of the universe.

We got out of the van and Godiva followed me to the door. Catskinner's vigilance was making me feel twitchy—he wanted control of my eyes. I wasn't ready to let him take over though. I wanted to check out the nest for myself.

The big front windows were full of movie posters in foreign languages, a lot of tough guys with guns and swooning girls with ripped dresses. It made me feel like a crowd of particularly anti-social shoppers were watching us.

"Do we just go in?" I wondered aloud.

Godiva shrugged. "Might as well."

The closer I got to the door the more agitated Catskinner became.

it is not safe here.

I sighed. He was probably right. I stopped walking. Let me do the talking? And don't kill anyone unless you have to?

agreed.

Usually when I let Catskinner take over I let myself sort of fade away. This time I deliberately stayed aware of what was going on around me. There was the familiar sense of distance from my body as Catskinner walked me up to the door, but I wasn't just a passive observer. Whatever happened here, I would be part of it.

I could tell that Godiva sensed Catskinner take over, and I tried to turn to face her. After a moment, Catskinner moved my head so I could see her.

"It's okay." I said, and my voice sounded strange in my ears. I wasn't hearing it though the bones of my skull, I realized, but only with my ears. "I'm still here."

My body walked to the door and my eyes scanned the area all around it. Catskinner didn't focus on objects the way I did. My eyes seemed to be registering the shape of the empty space as if it was more important. Maybe for him it was.

Beside me Godiva took a deep breath, but Catskinner didn't turn to her, he just pushed on the door—I could feel how careful he was not to break it—and walked inside.

It was dark inside, or at least darker than the bright sunlight outside, and then it wasn't. All at once the store went from dim to bright. Instinctively I tried to glance at the overhead lights, but my head moved slowly side to side and didn't look up. Catskinner had adjusted my eyes, I realized.

The inside of the store was one big room, but it didn't seem to be as big as it should have been from the outside and I guessed part of the space was walled off.

Music was playing, bright and cheerful and little relentless. A young girl's voice in what I guessed was Japanese. To me it sounded like she was singing "oochi boochi woochi" over and over again.

People. A man in a polo shirt and jeans pawing through a rack of CDs or DVDs—Catskinner kept my eyes moving too quickly to get a good look.

A middle aged woman, Asian and thin as a rail, in a white blouse and standing, I realized as my eyes slid past her, behind the counter.

Another woman, wild mass of auburn hair, black tank top showing pale skin, idly spinning a rack of jewelry, gold and silver sparkling against white plastic.

Catskinner walked me to the counter, my head still swiveling back and forth like a scanning camera. I caught a quick glimpse of Godiva walking beside me. Another man, young, in a black leather jacket, looked up from poking through a display of T-shirts to watch us go past.

Three customers, one employee? I asked in my head. It was hard to keep track without being able to move my head for myself.

four, was all he replied.

We reached the counter. The Asian woman looked harmless, but Catskinner stiffened and I felt his awareness ratchet up to red alert.

Well. "Hello," I said. Again my voice sounded like a bad recording.

I realized I also sounded like an idiot, but that wasn't Catskinner's fault.

The woman looked at me for a moment, waiting to see if I would say anything else. When I didn't she asked, "What brings the butcher to our door?"

The butcher? Oh, yes, that would be me, or Catskinner, really. "I've come to talk about Keith Morgan," I said.

I heard the front door open and close. *five*, Catskinner said in my head.

The counter woman was still looking at me. Yeah, okay, I said I was here to say something about him, I probably should think of something to say.

Godiva rescued me. "We want you to stop doing business with him."

The woman glanced at her briefly, then back at me.

"If we do this, you will not kill us?" Another door—not the front one, but behind the counter someplace—opened and closed. *six and seven*, Catskinner told me. I could feel that he was keeping track of everyone else in the store, but I wasn't sure how, since he kept my eyes focused on the woman we were talking to.

"Uh . . . yeah, that's the basic idea." I tried smiling at her, but it didn't work very well.

"Agreed."

Agreed? Was it really that simple?

"Okay, good." I said. I tried to look over at Godiva, but Catskinner wouldn't shift his attention.

Godiva leaned forward. "You're willing to stop trading with Morgan, just like that?" She seemed surprised as well.

The woman's attention shifted to Godiva. "You and Keith Morgan are in conflict. It is in our best interest to avoid that conflict. We have sufficient stockpiles to last until the conflict is ended, at which time we can negotiate with the survivor."

Reasonable. Cold, but reasonable.

"I also want to know who else Morgan trades with," I said.

The woman looked down at the counter. There was a newspaper there, not in English. Chinese, if I had to guess. She picked up the paper and started paging through it, just as if Godiva and I weren't standing right in front of her.

"And how is that in our best interest?" someone asked. A male voice, and I was suddenly facing him. It was the guy in the polo shirt who had been looking through the DVDs. Not a customer, I realized, but part of the nest.

"It will keep me from killing you," I pointed out.

Everyone in the store was looking at us, and I realized that there were no customers. They were all part of the nest.

The redhead in the black tank top spoke up. "My hosts are replaceable. My relations with the others of my kind are more difficult to repair."

I couldn't think of any way to argue with that, and Catskinner still wasn't letting me look at Godiva. I could hear her sigh, though.

"What would be in your best interest to tell us?"

"Goodbye," said the young man in the black leather jacket, from where he stood by the T-shirt display. He didn't make any move to usher us out though. He just stood there, unnaturally still. I was beginning to see how unnerving Catskinner must seem to ordinary people. Now that the nestlings had dropped their pretense of humanity they stood like a collection of manikins.

"What about those of your kind that you don't have such a good relationship with?" I pressed them. "Don't try to tell me that everything from the great beyond is sweetness and light and you all just love each other to death—I know better. Something out there gave Morgan the idea to kill Victor."

"We don't know who." From the one who had come in the store when I was facing away from the door, a white haired, round faced man in a black suit.

"No, but I bet you know somebody you wouldn't mind me leaning on. Give us a name, and we'll go away. Otherwise—" I still didn't have a clear plan for otherwise, but it turned out I didn't need one. Catskinner spun me around again and I saw the Asian woman holding out a slip of paper from behind the counter.

"MacNuth," she said. "MacNuth Intermodel Freight Forwarding. On Hall street."

"What's their connection to Morgan?" Godiva asked.

"That's where he keeps money. Cash in large amounts. We have made deliveries for him," from the redhead.

"Good. Thank you." I tried to turn, instead Catskinner stepped neatly backwards, my head scanning back and forth. Godiva backed up as well, nodding thoughtfully. We walked to the door and they didn't say another word. They just watched me, seven faces with the same blank expression.

Well, they'd already said goodbye.

Catskinner walked me backwards three more steps and then withdrew, pouring out of my body. I sagged, nearly stumbled, feeling suddenly weak. Godiva put her hand on my arm.

I shook my head. "I'm okay."

"He takes a lot out of you," she said, concerned.

I nodded. "Yeah. I just need some food."

Then a man walked around the corner of the store with a gun in his hand.

Chapter Thirteen

"as plants are food for animals and animals are food for men, so must men be food for angels"

He was a big man, with a dark crewcut and a dark suit and looked just like what he yelled at us, which was "Federal agent!" then "Keep your hands where I can see them."

Catskinner bristled, but the gun was not actually pointed at us and I was able to keep him from taking over. My body was already drained. I didn't want to stress it any more unless I had to.

"Okay," I sighed. "What do you want?"

He was holding his gun to the side, pointed down. He held up his other hand in a stop gesture. "First, my partner is behind your van. He's also armed. We have a pretty good idea what you can do, and we aren't taking any chances. We just want to talk."

i can kill them both.

Before one of them shoots Godiva?

. . .

I thought so. Let them talk first.

"Okay. I'm listening." Beside me Godiva was very still.

"I'm Tom White. My partner back there is Corbett Russwin."

"Okay." I wasn't planning on introducing myself.

Godiva was looking back at the van. "Hey," she called out. "You—Russwin—get out where we can see you."

I glanced back. The man who stepped around the van looked pretty much like White, except his crewcut was blond. He had a gun in his hand, too, and his was also pointed at the ground. Godiva started walking to the van, guiding me with her hand on my arm.

"We just want to talk," White repeated.

"We'll talk in the middle of the lot," Godiva countered. "Where we can all see each other."

"Fair enough," Russwin said agreeably. He backed up.

Godiva followed him, and I followed her, and White followed me. We went across the lot like that, a game of slow motion follow-the-leader. There was a big white sedan parked away from the other cars, pointing out. Russwin backed up to it and leaned on the hood, his gun in plain sight, pointed at the ground.

"This okay?" Russwin asked. His voice was low and calm, with a hint of some rural accent.

Godiva nodded. "Sure. Mr. White, how about you join your partner?"

White made a large circle around us and backed up to the back of the car. "Okay, now could you please tell us what you are doing here?"

Godiva grinned at him. "Shopping."

White shook his head. "I don't believe you."

Godiva turned to Russwin. "What federal agency do you two work for, exactly?"

"State Department."

"Uh huh. Got some ID?"

Russwin reached carefully into his jacket and pulled out a wallet. He flipped it open. Godiva leaned forward and spat in his face.

The effect was electric. Russwin cursed and began clawing at his eyes with his free hand. His gun was waving all over the place. I felt Catskinner surge forward and I let him go, and then the gun was in my hand. White started to bring his gun up, and then it was in my other hand and White was on the ground behind their car.

"Nobody move!" I shouted, and felt Catskinner retreat—a little—as I said it. White lifted his hands without getting up.

Russwin was still rubbing his face. I stood there with a gun in each hand.

"Hey," White said. "Let's just all relax a little, all right? Take a deep breath. Cobb, are you okay?"

"She spit acid in my face!" He sounded upset, but not injured.

"It's allyl isothiocyanate, actually," Godiva explained, which explained nothing. Realizing that, she added, "It's the active ingredient in horseradish."

I stared at her. "You didn't eat any horseradish," I objected.

"My body can synthesize—that's not important right now. He'll be fine, it just hurts."

"Damn right it does," Russwin muttered bitterly.

"It's okay, though, right?" White was speaking very slowly and a little too calm. "Nobody's hurt, right? Nobody has to do anything drastic."

I was in favor of not doing anything drastic. Federal agents were cops, and cops never stop looking for people who do drastic things to other cops.

"Okay. . ." I thought for a few seconds. "How about I throw the guns behind the store, and then we take off and you forget you ever saw us?"

"Works for me," Russwin growled. He'd stopped rubbing his face and sounded better.

"No!" Godiva objected. "Not until we get some answers."

White propped himself up on his elbows. "Okay, ask away."

Russwin dropped his hands. His face was red and blotchy. "Tom . . ."

White sighed. "Yes, Cobb, I know."

"I'm just saying. . . ."

White turned his head to look up to where his partner leaned against the car. "You were right, and I was wrong. Are you happy now?"

"Not really." Russwin looked at Godiva. "What do you want to know?"

"What are you two doing here?"

"Surveillance," White said, as if the answer should have been obvious.

"On whom?"

They paused on that one, shared a glance. Russwin fielded it. "We have intelligence that indicates this location may be used by agents of a foreign power."

"How foreign?" I asked. "I mean, you're not talking about France or Norway here, right? Agents of someplace a lot farther away?"

Godiva shot me a warning glance, but I figured they already knew more than most people or they wouldn't be here.

A slow thoughtful nod from Russwin, then; "Yeah. Very foreign agents."

"So the government knows about . . . the outsiders?"

Russwin looked down at the ground, "Well, I wouldn't say—"

White interrupted him quickly. "We can't comment on that."

Interesting. I looked down at the guns. I was still holding one in each hand. They were getting heavy but I didn't want to set them down. They were identical chrome automatics. I didn't know much about guns, but they looked like cop guns to me.

"Why does your car have New Mexico plates?" Godiva asked suddenly. I looked at the back of the car—I hadn't noticed before, but she was right.

That caught them off guard. "It's what we were issued," White said, but he didn't sound convincing. Russwin sighed, still looking at the ground.

"You're not really federal agents," Godiva said.

Russwin looked up at her. "Actually, we really are. The situation is, uh—"

"Kind of fluid," White finished for him.

"Non-conventional" Russwin added.

"Ad hoc," from White.

"We operate primarily as inter-agency liaisons," Russwin concluded.

Godiva raised her eyebrows. "Really. Between which agencies?"

"Well," White began, "you have to realize that there is a considerable degree of jurisdictional latitude within the federal system—"

"If something were to happen to you two right now, who would come looking for you?" Godiva asked.

Another shared look. "The Bureau, of course, it'd be their jurisdiction," from Russwin.

"So if I called the local FBI office right now they'd be able to confirm that you're federal agents?"

"Now, I couldn't say that the local duty officer would be in a position to provide confirmation, as such," from White.

"There are procedures, you know. Channels." Russwin added.

"It might take some time to process a request like that." White again. "Days. Weeks, even."

I was getting tired of them, and the guns were still heavy. "I bet they work for Morgan."

Everybody got really quiet.

"Morgan?" White asked slowly.

"I knew a Joanna Morgan at BIA in Oklahoma City," Russwin ventured.

"Keith Morgan." I said, "Here in town. He wants to kill me, and I think you work for him."

"No." From White.

"Absolutely not." From Russwin.

Godiva chewed her lip. "No, I think they're just con men."

"Now wait just a minute," White seemed genuinely indignant. "We do a lot of important work. You know—you know damn well—that there are things out there that most of the human race is not prepared to deal with. That includes law enforcement on every level. We provide intelligence that allows agencies to make informed decisions. Intelligence that saves lives."

"You lie to them." Godiva interpreted.

"We tell them what they'll believe." Russwin didn't sound angry, just old and very tired. "You figure if we told Interstate Commerce that this video piracy operation here was run by some kind of hive mind organism using human hosts they'd take it seriously? Instead we say it's a Ukrainian mob and exaggerate the numbers a little, play up the human trafficking and brainwashing angles. We tell them what's going to give them a fighting chance to survive what they're walking into."

"That still doesn't explain who you're working for," Godiva pointed out.

"I like to think that we're working for the human race," White said.

I sighed. More knights. "Yeah, you and Alice."

Russwin stiffened. "Alice? Alice who?"

Godiva rolled her eyes at me. I shrugged—I'm just not cut out for covert ops.

"You're talking about Alice Mason, aren't you?" White growled. "What have you done with her?"

"Relax," Godiva spread her hands, "Alice is a common name."

White dropped to the ground and rolled under the car.

Catskinner jerked my body to follow but I fought him. From under the car I heard a metallic slide and click. A very weapon-like sound.

"Yes, Alice Mason, but she's fine!" I shouted. It was all I could do to hold Catskinner back. "We're working with her—I'm not going to hurt her!"

"Bullshit!" from White under the car. "Mason doesn't work with OTH assets."

OTH? I wondered, and then Catskinner surged up like a wave and I was swept away. I was on top of the car and then sliding down the hood and then Russwin was in my arms, his hands pinioned at his sides. Catskinner had dropped the gun in my left hand. I wasn't sure when.

"throw out the shotgun now or i rip out his heart."

"Let him go or I shoot your girlfriend's legs off!" White countered.

Don't let Godiva get hurt, I silently begged Catskinner.

i won't. trust me.

"Everybody!" Godiva hollered, "Just! Calm! The! Fuck! Down!"

Catskinner was half facing the road. In my peripheral vision I could see traffic continuing to flow up and down Manchester road. People just drove right by our little drama. People see what they want to see.

Godiva took a deep breath. "White, Alice Mason was fine when we left her this morning. Russwin, why don't you call her and ask her about us? Catskinner, let Russwin go so he can make the call. He's not a threat to you."

"the other one is."

"The shotgun's pointed at me, not you. I'm the one taking the risk. Let him go." Godiva was speaking very slowly and carefully.

i don't like this.

Me, either, but she's right. Let him go, and maybe we can avoid any more violence.

Catskinner released Russwin, but he kept control of my body. I was starting to really worry about my blood sugar reserves.

Russwin faced Catskinner. "I'm going to get my phone out now." He reached slowly into his jacket pocket and came out with a phone.

"mr. white if you shoot godiva i will skin both of you."

"Understood." from under the car.

Russwin paged through the numbers on his phone and selected one. I could hear it ring, then—

"Alice. Hi, it's Cobb Russwin. Look, we've got kind of a situation here."

A pause. I could hear that Alice was talking, but couldn't catch the words.

"Well, we've run across a couple of folks that say they know you—" Another pause.

"Yeah, that's them, all right."

A big white truck was slowing as it approached the entrance to the parking lot. I probably wouldn't have noticed it, but Catskinner did and he moved my head to follow it.

Russwin chuckled, then said, "I'll tell him that." Louder; "Tom, Alice says stop being such a dick."

From under the car White started saying, "Look, you tell her—" but I missed the rest because the white truck turned into the lot and began accelerating towards us, and Catskinner let go of Russwin and launched me towards it.

My feet were hitting the windshield and going through it in a shower of glass before I got a good look at the driver, and then Catskinner threw him out of the cab.

drive. now.

And I was in the driver's seat, both figuratively and literally. Catskinner couldn't handle machines, something about the concept of indirect action was beyond him. I grabbed the steering wheel and spun it. I didn't have time to try to find the pedals, and it was headed straight for the car.

Evidently big trucks don't corner so well at high speed. I could tell that it was tipping, but there wasn't a hell of a lot I could do except try to hang on. All the loose trash in the cab—fast food wrappers, coffee cups, random tools—came at me.

i didn't expect you to crash it.

I didn't have a lot of choice.

There was a whole lot of noise and a whole lot of glass, and then I was lying on my side against what was left of the driver's side window with the wind knocked out of me and new set of bruises pretty much everywhere.

Chapter Fourteen

"for all things that live and must one day die, weep tears of blood. for all that dies and first must live, weep tears of iron."

The motor was still running, ragged and choppy, so I reached up and turned the key until it stopped.

I started to get up. I hurt, but didn't seem to be badly injured anywhere. There was a lot of blood on the pavement, but it wasn't coming from me. I guessed the driver went under the wheel when Catskinner tossed him out of the cab. I'd missed White and Russwin's car, The truck lay on its side diagonally across the lot. The two feds—or psuedofeds, or whatever they were—stood behind the car, next to Godiva. They weren't threatening her, all three of them were looking at me.

I'd managed to mostly fill my lungs, so I tried calling to them. "I'm okay." I didn't sound convincing, even to myself.

"Get out of the truck!" Godiva hollered back, which is when I smelled something burning.

I didn't want to turn my body over to Catskinner until I had figured out just how badly I was worn down, but if I didn't move quickly he would take it. I got to my feet and stepped out through the shattered windshield. I was unsteady on feet, but vertical.

I was tottering towards the car when I heard something moving from the truck. It sounded like a chain being dragged across concrete and I felt a heat like the inside of an oven. Catskinner reached and I let him have control—I'd take exhaustion and some

118

pulled muscles over being incinerated.

Catskinner sprinted to the car and I saw that all three of them had guns—White had the shotgun that had been hidden under the car, Russwin and Godiva each had one of the automatics. Catskinner dropped and rolled, under the car and up on my feet on the other side, next to Godiva. Only then did I get a chance to see whatever they were all aiming at.

At first it looked like molten copper was pouring out of the back of the truck, waves of heat shimmers rising over it. But why would they be pointing guns at molten metal?

"What the hell are they?" Godiva hissed.

"Minraudim," White spat back.

He swung the shotgun and fired a half dozen rounds into the advancing mass. Instead of splashes, there was a confused tangle of lines that resolved themselves into legs and bits of shell, and all of a sudden I realized that I was looking at a swarm of centipedes— hot metal centipedes. The shotgun blasts had torn a whole in the swarm, but they closed ranks and kept coming.

White pulled open the car door and reached inside for more shells. Russwin emptied his gun into the swarm as White reloaded and after a moment Godiva did likewise. The bullets were killing individual centipedes—minraudim, White had called them—but there were far too many of them for killing them one at a time to save us.

Got any ideas? I asked Catskinner in my head.

"we should run," he said aloud.

"Great idea!" White agreed. He had the shotgun ready again, and swept it in an arc, firing another six shots. "Your van?"

Godiva was struggling with the gun, trying to get the clip out. Russwin grabbed her by the shoulder and pulled her towards the van. Catskinner spun me and I sprinted for the driver's door. He swung me inside and released me, and my vision went gray. I struggled to get the keys out of my pocket. I was drained.

Catskinner had pushed my body too far, too fast, with too little time to recover.

The others reached the van. Russwin was first through the door, I handed him the keys and struggled into the back.

"You drive," I managed to gasp out.

He took the keys and slid into the driver's seat, pushing me out of the way. I hit the floor and Godiva scrambled over to me. Russwin started the van and floored it as White was still climbing into the passenger seat. Godiva landed on me in a heap. She smelled nice, but it still hurt.

"James." Godiva pulled me so that I was lying on her more than the other way around. "What's wrong?"

Dimly I was aware of a blast of heat as the fed's car burst into flame. Russwin had gotten the van turned around and was heading down the alley behind the store. I hoped it led out to the street eventually.

"I'm just tired." I was losing consciousness. "He . . . ."

I felt her smooth small hands encircling my face and she pulled her face to mine. "Relax," she whispered. "Just take it." And then her lips were against mine. She still had her teeth in, and I could feel how they didn't quite fit, that more was moving in her mouth than just her tongue. I could taste sweetness on her lips.

Then something in her chest heaved and my mouth was suddenly full of something thick and sweet. Shocked, I started to choke and then swallowed it. Her chest heaved again and she fed me more of it, it was warm and tasted faintly of mint.

"Oh, fergoodnesssake!" I heard White's disgusted mutter from the front seat. I opened my eyes.

Godiva pulled back her face from mine and I drew in a long breath.

"Better?" she asked softly.

I realized it was better. Whatever she'd produced for me must have been nearly pure glucose sugar, and I felt energy returning.

"Yes," I said. "Thank you."

She smiled at me, then turned to White. "We need to stop and get some food."

"Now?" Russwin asked irritably.

"As soon as possible," I said. "Catskinner—my outsider friend—burns a lot of calories."

"Makes sense," White said grudgingly. Then to Russwin, "We've got time—no one's going to follow us out of that."

I managed to sit up enough to look out the window. The entire store that had housed the nest was engulfed in flames. The sky was dark with smoke.

"Morgan," I said. "He figured if they wouldn't work for him—"

"Then they won't be working for anyone," White agreed. "He's a son of a bitch, all right."

The alley reached a cross street at the end and Russwin turned onto it, headed back to Manchester. There was a fast food place on the corner.

"This do you?" Russwin asked.

"Sure," I said. "Get me one of everything, and supersize it."

We ordered through the drive-thru and then parked in the lot. While I engulfed forty bucks worth of burgers and fries Godiva talked strategy with Russwin and White. I didn't really listen. I had already decided to go along with whatever she wanted to do. She was clearly smarter than I was, and besides, I had another conversation to listen that was more important.

You could have killed us.

the fire arachnids would have done so.

Granted. Still, I don't want to cut it that close again.

we should keep food in the van.

Also granted. You also need to be more aware of how my body is doing.

i can keep the body safe.

So can I. You can't be out all the time. You have to trust me.

i trust you. i don't trust the world.

Do you trust Godiva?

i don't trust the world.

She saved our life.

That reminded me of something. I turned to Godiva. "Do you want some food? I mean, do you need it after . . . doing that?"

She shook her head. "I'm okay."

"How about you guys?" I asked the two agents. "You want anything? I'm buying."

A grunt from White. Russwin said, "Yeah, I could use a soda. Something with caffeine in it."

White said, "Yeah, now that you mention it, me, too. It's been a long day."

"I'll be right back." I slid open the sliding door and stepped out. Catskinner was aware, his attention radiating all around me, but I didn't feel it focused on anything in particular and he wasn't trying to take control.

I thought about what he said as I crossed the lot to the restaurant.

i trust you. i don't trust the world.

I had to admit he had a point.

Once I got back to the van with the sodas, they had decided what to do next. We were going to head up to the bowling alley and meet with Alice again. Some plan. I could have thought of that one myself.

I was feeling better, so I told Russwin to get out of the way and let me drive. He got in the back with Godiva.

Alice was already sitting at a big table in the back when we got there. White volunteered to fetch drinks while the rest of us joined her.

"Okay, so what happened?" Alice began.

Godiva looked over at Russwin. He nodded and gave Alice a brief rundown of the events.

"Any chance that it wasn't Morgan who sent those things?"

Alice asked when he was done.

Godiva frowned. "I suppose it's possible. . . ."

White had come back by that point. "Who else would make a blatant move like that against the Manchester nest?" he asked.

"Wait—" I objected. "You figure the nest was the target? I thought they were after us."

"They were," White agreed. "But using minraudim is like using a nuke—you have to expect collateral damage. Even if you hadn't killed their handler, they would have still burned the nest. They burn everything in their path."

"And now they're loose in West County?" That didn't sound good at all.

Russwin shook his head. "They don't live long in this environment. It's too cold—even with all the fires they set. Odds are they are already dead and reverted."

"Reverted?" Another new word.

Alice explained. "Most exobiotics are inherently unstable. They don't belong in this universe. It's like . . . holding a balloon underwater, it takes energy to keep them here. Once the energy is gone, they sort of fall apart."

I consider that. "Like the dish soap thing?"

"Exactly."

"What's OTH mean?" Godiva asked White suddenly.

He stared at her. "Huh?"

"Before your partner called Alice you said she never works with OTH assets. What did you mean by that?"

Russwin leaned over the table. "Other Than Human," he explained softly. "No offense, but the two of you are."

Godiva turned to Alice and raised her eyebrows.

"I do not work with 'assets', I work with people," Alice said angrily. She turned her glare to White. "And yes, I do work with people who have been altered."

White didn't seem at all uncomfortable. "It's not your usual

MO. Considering this guy's rep"—he nodded in my direction—"I figured the odds were against you having a conversation with him and staying healthy."

"And yet here I am," Alice pointed out.

"And here I am, too." I was starting to find White really annoying. "This guy doesn't just slaughter everyone he meets, you know."

White turned to me. "Maybe not every single person, no."

"James, like it or not, you are a very dangerous man," Russwin said. "Threat assessment deals with capabilities, not intentions."

That reminded me of something. "Alice, you know these two?"

She nodded. "We've worked together in the past."

"Are they really federal agents?"

Alice gave a wry smile. "They're campers."

"Campers?" Godiva was looking interested, too.

"Basically they find an empty office in a federal building and move in." Alice explained.

I stared at the men. "Does that work?"

"She's oversimplifying," Russwin said.

White frowned. "We arrange for lateral transfers into temporarily understaffed positions."

Godiva grinned. "And no one ever questions who sent you?"

"All it takes is an understanding of how the bureaucracy operates and fair amount of chutzpa," Alice continued. "When a department needs help and someone shows up to work, most people aren't going to look too hard at the paperwork."

"As I said earlier, Russwin and I are specialists. We bring a unique understanding of certain lesser acknowledged phenomenon to our assignments." White took a drink of his soda. "We go where there is a need."

Godiva raised an eyebrow. "Uh-huh."

Russwin stood up. "Thanks for the lift, but I think my partner and I have work to do. See you around."

White sighed and stayed where he was. "Sit down, Cobb," he said. "I think it's a little late to just walk away."

Russwin shook his head. "I don't think this is our fight, Tom."

Godiva looked up at him. "Please, Mr. Russwin. We could use your help."

Russwin sat back down. "What kind of help?"

"Information, mostly. What can you tell us about Morgan?"

Russwin sighed. "He's mid-thirties, born in Chicago, moved here to go to school. Started as a math major, moved to education, then dropped out. He's got a record, all little stuff. Shoplifting, misdemeanor possession, a credit card fraud charge that was later dismissed. About ten years ago he started making big money as a day trader. Then he fell off the grid. No bank accounts, no tax returns, no driver's license, no vehicle registration—nothing. Just vanished."

Godiva frowned. "What about The Good Earth?"

White picked it up. "On paper it's owned by a 501c3 nonprofit called The Good Earth Food Co-Op. It doesn't have any employees, and the officers are just names and post office boxes. We know Morgan owns it, and a bunch of other crap, but we can't prove it."

"Post office boxes," I mused. "Someone has to pick up the mail, right? I mean, they get official documents and stuff there."

"A messenger service," Alice interjected. "I looked into that, it's a dead end."

I frowned. "He can't get everything delivered."

"Actually, he can," White said.

Godiva shook her head. "There has got to be some way to draw him out. Something that he'll have to deal with in person."

"Look, maybe we're thinking about this all wrong—" I started.

Everybody looked at me expectantly. Oh, right, now I was supposed to explain what thinking about it all right would be. Unfortunately, I didn't have any clear idea.

"Are we sure that we can't come to some kind of arrangement?

I mean, does this have to be about killing somebody?" I tried.

Russwin leaned back, folded his arms. "Honestly, I never expected you to be advocating restraint."

"And what's that supposed to mean?" I didn't like his tone.

"Well, from what I know about you—" he started.

I didn't let him finish. "You don't know anything about me."

He cocked his head. "Actually, we do. James Ozryck, known associate of Victor Sells, aka Victor Scziller, aka Viktor Szeck," Russwin handled the Eastern European names better than I did, "suspected involvement in no fewer than seventy counts of murder one. You're a killer for hire, and a damned good one."

I looked down at my hands. "You don't know anything about me," I repeated.

Russwin kept going. "Believed also to be Adam Chase, which if true would put the count closer to a hundred and fifty."

I looked up and met his eyes. "I have never killed anyone," I said softly.

An exaggerated eye-roll. "Oh, that's right, it's not you, it's that thing inside you. Well, you know something, it doesn't make one damn bit of difference to me."

"That's because you're an idiot," Godiva blurted out.

Russwin glared at her. White stifled a snort.

Godiva refused to back down. "Well, you are. It makes a huge difference. How long did it take Catskinner to take your gun away? Half a second? Why do you think he didn't go ahead and kill you? Because James isn't a killer—and that's why you're alive right now."

Russwin opened his mouth, but White interrupted him. "She's right, you know."

Russwin turned to White, frowned, then nodded slowly. He turned back to me. "Okay, fair enough. You"—he emphasized the word— "would rather not kill Morgan. But Catskinner can and will."

"*and wants to,*" Catskinner's voice just came out. I hadn't known he was even listening.

"Right." Russwin looked carefully at my face, and I could see him seeing the differences. "Well, maybe we should be talking to you, then."

My eyes turned to Godiva. *"he is not an idiot."*

"Well, no, not literally," Godiva allowed, "Technically, an idiot has the mental capacity of a four year old."

My eyes flickered back to Russwin. *"it is hard for you to kill your own kind. you are frightened of james because you think it is easy for james to kill his own kind. you are wrong. james does not kill. i kill, and it is easy for me because humans are not my kind."*

And then he was gone, leaving me facing Russwin's eyes—eyes that looked me like I was an infectious disease.

"You're right," I told him, "this is not your fight."

"Now, let's just wait a minute—" White objected.

"You said it yourself," I reminded him, "Other Than Human. What do you care what happens to me and Godiva?"

"I care because you can keep me alive," White shot back. "Look, I get it—you're tired of being treated like a monster and you want somebody to like you for you. And, believe me, I'd love to be able to say that I think you're a sweet guy and I'll invite you to my daughter's quinceañera, but you and I both know I'd be lying. But that doesn't matter. What does matter is that you saved me from being burned alive—as far as I'm concerned that puts you on the side of the angels."

White directed a pointed look at Russwin. "Now if we can all just put our egos away for a few minutes, let's talk about how we can all work together to stay healthy."

Russwin glanced at White, nodded, then turned back to me. "Sorry," he said. "I didn't understand."

I nodded. Was I supposed to apologize to him now? "It's confusing," I admitted. That was as close as I could get.

That seemed to satisfy him. He leaned back in his chair and

looked over at Alice. "So what now?"

She sighed deeply. "Well, the usual strategy against someone who is holed up is a siege. But I don't see us having time for that—I'm sure he's got reserves."

Something occurred to me. "What about his power?"

"He's been consolidating his forces for years—" Alice began.

I waved my hands to cut her off, and Russwin flinched. Sorry. "No, no, I mean his electric power."

They looked at me.

"I didn't see a generator in that place. He's on the city power, right?"

White nodded slowly. "Yeah, his utilities are paid from a Good Earth account. Electric, gas, water, sewer, all the usuals."

"So we can cut his power lines," I suggested. "That might get a reaction."

Russwin frowned. "You can't just cut down high tension wires."

White agreed. "And if you did, Ameren UE would just put them back up. He wouldn't have to leave the shop."

Godiva cocked her head. "Have you guys got any pull with the utility companies?"

A pause. Then, "Not as such," from Russwin, but slowly, like he was thinking it over.

White looked over at him. "We could maybe get a grand jury to freeze the account temporarily..."

Russwin shook his head. "Too slow. We'd need to do it from a public safety angle."

"What township is that?" Godiva asked.

"Unincorporated county," Alice answered her.

"Still?"

"Yeah," White said. "There's about six blocks in there that are still unincorporated. I get the feeling that he likes it that way."

Russwin nodded slowly, thinking it over. "County Fire, then. We can work with them."

I remembered something. "When I was there, he said the fire inspectors didn't know he existed."

"Interesting," White said, "Let's see what we can do about that. Maybe HUD?"

Russwin nodded. "I was thinking Census, but HUD might work better."

I wasn't quite following the discussion, even though I had kind of started it. "So, you can use HUD to shut off his electricity?"

"Not exactly," White countered, "but utility customers are required to be in compliance with certain federal, state, and local ordinances, which, in turn are interpreted by the local authority having jurisdiction, who in this case would be County Fire. Now, County Fire has a vested interest in maintaining the good will of Housing and Urban Development, and would be inclined to cooperate, eh, vigorously, with an ongoing investigation into a fraud case involving the misapprehension of federal funds."

"Which the Good Earth does not receive," Alice pointed out.

"Not directly, no," Russwin allowed, "however, as a 501c3—"

"IRS," White said.

"Great, who gets to swim with the sharks?" Russwin sighed.

"Flip you for it," White suggested.

"You can get his utilities shut off?" Godiva asked.

White looked at Russwin. Russwin looked at White, then over to Godiva. "Tomorrow's Monday. I'm thinking Wednesday, can you survive until Wednesday?"

Catskinner answered for all of us. *"yes."*

Alice nodded slowly. "That should work."

"What the hell—?" Godiva was looking over White's shoulder.

Chapter Fifteen

"death is the cessation of appetite."

I turned slowly. Whatever was going on hadn't triggered Catskinner's threat radar, his attention stayed focused on Russwin and White. At first I couldn't tell what Godiva was looking at.

Things seemed normal, for a bowling alley on a Sunday afternoon. About half of the lanes were in use and nobody looked like they were taking it too seriously—not the hushed concentration of a league night. An ordinary crowd, jeans and T-shirts, the bowling an excuse to eat junk food and drink beer on a Sunday afternoon. But then I noticed a group coming in the door that wasn't ordinary.

My first thought was "beach volleyball team." But this wasn't Southern California. Firm young bodies in tight shorts and tank tops, white against tanned skin. Bright smiles and flowing hair, pink lipstick and fingernails.

And every one of them was wearing sunglasses.

Godiva stood up. Russwin and White reflexively flanked their hands on their holsters, looking more confused than concerned. Even Catskinner didn't see the new arrivals as a threat.

Nor did the patrons of the bowling alley.

The group of young women spread out from the entrance, smiling warmly. It looked like an advertising gimmick. I expected them to start handing out fliers or free samples of hair care products. Obviously Godiva expected something different.

"Don't let them get close," she said to White and Russwin. "They spit."

Russwin gave her a sharp look, then nodded, turning his attention back to the newcomers. They were joining the small groups that occupied the lanes, introducing themselves and joining in the conversations. I saw, or felt, an echo of Catskinner's perceptions of their movements as a strategic infiltration and his focus warmed my back. None of them approached us, but I started to share Godiva's concern.

"Who are they?" I asked Alice softly.

"They're ambimorphs," she answered, watching them warily. "But what are they doing here?"

Oh yes, of course. Ambimorphs. That explained . . . nothing. Still, whatever they were had Godiva concerned. I stood up. "Okay, so, I'm going to take a wild guess and say it's time to go."

Alice stood and we started moving towards the exit. A lean young woman—ambimorph—was sitting on the counter by the door, her athletic legs stretched out. The counterman was untying her sneakers, a goofy grin on his face. Neither of them so much as looked up as we passed, but I noticed Russwin had his gun out, holding down by his leg, and White kept his hand on his holster.

Somebody started clapping, rhythmically and I jumped. One of the ambimorphs had climbed on a table and was starting to dance surrounded by a wide-eyed crowd. This was getting really creepy.

"I can't believe he sent them to try and stop us," Godiva muttered, sounding disgusted.

"He didn't," said a new voice. A man was standing in the front lobby. A big man, muscular, with a shiny bald head, blocking the doors. "They're just here to pacify the crowd. I'm here to take you away."

White stopped and spread his arms slightly. "There's no reason this has to turn ugly. Just get out of the way and we'll be gone."

The bald man shrugged. "Sure, go ahead. You two can take off, or stay here and play with the girlies, or, heck, bowl a couple of frames. I don't care." He pointed at me and Godiva. "It's those two who are coming with me."

"we go nowhere at your bidding, hired man." Catskinner had slid into my body like a hand into a glove, smoothly filling the spaces between my nerve endings. I felt White and Russwin close ranks to either side of me, and Godiva slip behind us. Catskinner didn't turn to watch the others—maybe he was learning to trust them, or maybe he just saw the big man blocking the exit as the greater threat.

The bald man sighed. He wasn't just bald, I noticed, he had no hair at all, not even eyelashes. His skin looked slick and a little gray, almost like a dolphin's hide. He raised a hand and Catskinner's attention followed it. He had no fingernails, either. "Okay, I guess it does have to get ugly."

White had his gun out, pointed at the bald man. "Or maybe just for you."

For a moment we all just stood there, looking at each other. A long moment, long enough for me to think that maybe he was bluffing and that we were going to be able to just walk past him—

—and then things got really busy.

Somebody's gun went off, painfully loud, but I was in motion, past and over the gunshot, bouncing up to the ceiling. There was a huge ugly light fixture up there, some relic of the 1960s in chrome and neon with little ray gun projections all over it. I'd walked under it without noticing it, but evidently Catskinner had been paying attention because he yanked on it and it came crashing down—along with about half of the ceiling—to bury big and bald under a mess of debris. A regular human would have been crushed but he stood there unmoved and I felt Catskinner's realization of that fact along with an impression of terrible weight.

Catskinner was still moving across the lobby, and I heard more gunshots, one and two and three and four and five, calm and measured, then the sound of something big breaking. Then a fire extinguisher—something else I hadn't noticed but Catskinner had—was in my hands and I spun around and it impacted against the stranger in an explosion of white powder and smoke and still the bastard wouldn't go down, just staggered a little.

A bowling ball came out of somewhere and bounced off that bald head with no reaction. I guessed that either Godiva or Alice had thrown it, Russwin was standing back and changing clips, no expression on his face. White was down in a splash of blood at the stranger's feet.

What is that guy? I asked Catskinner in my head.

his elements have been shifted downwards, I heard in reply as my body hopped, dropped, rolled, and came up on my feet next to a rack of balls, *heavier metals than human bodies possess.*

Then my hands were throwing bowling balls. I knew how Catskinner could use my muscles. Those balls would have dented a battleship's hull, yet the stranger was still standing. I did, however, seem to have gotten his attention. He turned and started walking towards me.

I had mixed feelings about that.

Catskinner stood to face him, his attention fixed on the empty space around him. I saw Godiva bending over White. Russwin had reloaded but wasn't firing, I guess my body was in his line of sight. I didn't see Alice anywhere.

Catskinner was moving my head, scanning the surroundings. Something registered to one side, a flat metal panel on the wall, and then the stranger was on me and Catskinner ghosted out of the way of his strike.

See that metal sheet on the wall? I spoke in my head. See if you can get him to hit it.

Catskinner didn't reply, he was dodging, but my body moved against the wall.

"i will see you drowned deep in cold water," Catskinner spoke aloud,

and the bald man lunged at us. I was on the ground suddenly and there was a flash of white that blinded me, followed by the sound of something heavier than a man hitting the tile.

Through purple afterimages I saw Russwin growing closer and I took my body back. Catskinner gave it up easily.

"Is he down?" I asked Russwin. I still couldn't see well enough to tell.

"He's down," Russwin said. Evidently my plan had worked. The big guy swung at me and Catskinner dodged so that the big guy's fist went through the electrical panel instead. Whatever he was at least partially metallic.

My eyes were coming back but the place was mostly dark, emergency lights scattered here and there didn't do much to break the gloom. The place had grown eerily silent. The patrons were sitting quietly in the darkness. Even the clapping had stopped.

I turned to Godiva and White, sitting together on the floor. Godiva turned to me. White didn't.

"We need to get him to a hospital," she said simply. Alice was standing beside them. I hadn't noticed when she arrived.

Russwin bent to pull White to a standing position and Godiva stopped him with a yell.

"Careful!" A deep breath. "His skull is crushed. He's got subdural bleeding, bone fragments all through his parietal, he needs intubation, he needs—shit, he needs surgery now and I haven't got dick to work with!" She seemed on the verge of tears.

Russwin nodded slowly, and very gently drew White to his feet. Alice took his other side. White's legs hung loosely, unconnected with the ground, and his eyes were staring off into nothing.

That's when I heard the bald man getting up.

Catskinner spun me around. The stranger's clothes were burned, but his slick gray skin seemed unharmed. I reached to take control of my right arm, dug into my pocket for my keys.

"Take the van," I said, "get him to an ER." I tossed the keys behind me.

Catskinner walked my body forward and Russwin joined me. "*save your bullets for his eyes,*" Catskinner told him quietly, "*his eyes are soft.*"

The big man pointed at Russwin. "You—you can still get out of this. I've got no reason to hurt you." He was staggering a little, still looking dazed, but I had a feeling he was shaking off the effects of the shock.

"Not a chance, Tin Man," Russwin called back. "Not after what you did to my partner."

"He did shoot me," the other pointed out, "but, hey, suit yourself." He bent his back slightly and spread his arms like a wrestler.

Catskinner turned and ran.

He didn't run for the exit, but for the lanes.

After a moment I heard Tin Man following, and a moment after that Russwin followed him. We weren't running flat out, not as fast as I knew Catskinner could move.

We have a plan? I silently asked him.

yes.

Well, that was good to know.

Catskinner hopped up on a table and behind us baldy smashed through it. On the other side was an upholstered bench. On it two men—flannel shirts, jeans, ball caps—were locked in a passionate kiss, one of the pretty ambimorphs lying across both of their laps and smiling sweetly up at them. She jerked her head to follow me as Catskinner sped by, the men didn't notice our passing, even when our pursuer knocked the bench aside.

Up and over a rack of bowling balls and Catskinner lashed out with a kick that snapped one of the side supports. Balls rolled out onto the floor. I heard the big guy stumble and fall, smashing the tile floor. Catskinner spun in place, swung my arm at a table crowded with beer bottles and the air was full of flying glass. It didn't seem to faze the big man, he got up and we were running again. Up on the back of another bench, avoiding the gently moving bodies draped across it, and out onto the lane. Behind us the wood splintered with each step of our pursuer. Then a louder crack and the steps stopped.

Catskinner twisted to look behind. The man was shin deep in the floor, wrestling with the splintered wood of the lane. Catskinner grabbed a ball and hurled it. The man shot us a black look and ducked, catching the impact on his shoulder. He heaved himself up and got free of the wood, scrambling for purchase. Catskinner heaved another ball then ran again, heading back to the lobby.

A moment later the heavy steps were back in pursuit. Catskinner knocked over a vending machine without looking and I heard it smash under the other's footsteps. He wasn't moving as fast as he had been, we were wearing him down.

Catskinner slowed slightly—still moving faster than most unmodified humans could manage—and I felt the man behind us closing the gap.

Catskinner spun and leaped straight at the big man. Startled, he threw an arm up to block and Catskinner grabbed the arm and kicked out with both feet, swinging around his body like a tetherball. The big man's arm didn't break—

—it bent. Like an iron bar it flexed and bent in the middle of his upper arm, the bone twisted almost into a right angle. The big man's eyes got wide and his mouth opened to let out a long hiss of pain. He dropped to his knees, clutching his misshapen limb in his good arm. Catskinner pressed his advantage, lashing out with a half dozen rapid kicks to the man's face. We stepped back then. The big man blinked slowly and shook his head, trying to focus.

Russwin stepped up, put his gun against the man's eye, and fired three shots into his head. The big man fell straight back and I felt the floor crack under his weight. His one eye was simply gone, and the other bulged out. Blood mixed with a thick dark blue fluid poured out of his eyes and ears and mouth. The back of his skull was deformed, bulging out like a weak balloon.

Russwin switched to the other eye and fired three more shots into it. More blood and heavy blue gore sprayed across the floor.

He looked up at Catskinner. "Enough?"

"he's dead."

Russwin nodded and holstered his gun.

I took my body back, cautiously. I felt weak and the usual hunger, but it wasn't bad this time. The battle had gone faster than I realized.

I blinked, looked around. The ambimorphs were watching us silently. The patrons paid us no attention, lost in kissing and caressing each other, oblivious from whatever sexual spell had been cast on them.

I looked over at Russwin. He spoke to our audience of pretty girls. "We're leaving now, right? None of you are going to try to stop us, right?"

As one they turned from us and back to petting and murmuring to the patrons.

On the way out I reached behind the food counter—a teenage girl in a white apron lay on the tile floor, giggling softly, her hands between her legs—and helped myself to a couple of pieces of pizza.

Russwin made a call on his cell phone. No answer.

He frowned, tried another number. No answer.

"You got a number for Godiva?" he asked.

Mouth full, I shook my head.

He stood and thought for a while. "DePaul's closest. Let's go there."

He made another call, this one to a cab company.

I finished my pizza. "If they're in ICU they may not be able to use their phones," I suggested.

"Maybe," he seemed unconvinced.

They weren't at DePaul. No Tom White, no emergency room admissions of a middle-aged white male with a skull fracture.

Russwin showed some ID at the nurse's station and started asking questions. A few calls and a lot of searching on the nurse's computer told us that no one matching that description with those injuries had been admitted to any area hospital.

I felt sick. "He's got them."

Russwin nodded. "He must have had something else waiting outside." A long sigh. "We did just what he expected us to do."

"So where are they? The Good Earth?"

He pulled out his gun, pulled out the empty clip and replaced it with a full one before answering.

"No, I doubt it. He wouldn't want them that close to him."

I sat down on a hideous waiting room chair. "What do we do?" I asked softly.

"We need information. We need some bigger guns. We need a car." He pulled out his phone and called another cab.

"And then what?"

"Then we go hunting Mr. Morgan."

Chapter Sixteen

"all creation is also the destruction of what had been"

The cab took us to a dark industrial section of north city. A tall chain link fence topped with coils of razor wire surrounded a lot full of cars, most of them rusted hulks from what I could see. A faded steel sign warned "Entrance By Authorized Personnel Only," but didn't specify who did the authorizing.

I paid the driver in cash.

Russwin got out and held a quick conversation on his cell phone. A moment later there was a clink and a rattle and a section of the fence started rolling out of the way. Russwin entered the yard and I followed, Catskinner aware but not concerned by the neighborhood. Naturally. The most dangerous thing on the streets at night was him.

The gate began rattling closed behind us. Russwin seemed to know where he was going. There were aisles through the mass of vehicles and he turned right. I noticed that most of the cars seemed to be official vehicles of some kind—police cars, ambulances, an enormous fire truck that looked like it had been sitting there since World War II. At the end of the aisle was a big construction trailer with an illuminated sign in front of the office reading "Yard Office. Visitors MUST check in here."

The door to the trailer opened and a person headed down the metal steps, footsteps ringing in the quiet. A slim figure with a black leather jacket and a spiked mass of bright pink hair. Not what

I expected to see.

Russwin waved. "Hey, Ace."

The girl—Ace?—stopped and looked at me. "Hey, Cobb. Where's Tom? And who's the new guy?" She looked like a teenager, but then so did Godiva.

Is she human?

unmodified.

"Tom's out sick," Russwin said. "This is James, he's on loan from DEA."

Ace looked me over. "Nark, huh? Looks good. He doesn't look like a cop."

I held out my hand. "Pleased to meet you."

She grinned and took my hand. "Likewise." Then back to Russwin. "So, what can I do you for?"

"Wheels to start with," Russwin said.

"To start with, huh? Let's talk in the shack."

She led us up the stairs. The inside of the trailer seemed to be furnished with random items scavenged from government auctions. A half dozen chairs, two desks, some file cabinets, none of them matching, all of them ugly.

The computer system on one of the desks, on the other hand, looked new and powerful. It had two monitors, one of them showing views of the lot. There were movie posters on the walls, from horror movies I'd never heard of.

A coffeemaker sat on top of one of the filing cabinets, full, and Ace found some cups—also mismatched—and poured three cups. I didn't really want any, but I figured it was polite to take it and say "thank you."

Ace shrugged out of her jacket. Underneath she was wearing a black T-shirt that said, "Zombie Squad" under a logo of crossed machine guns.

"How are you fixed for vans?" Russwin asked.

Ace considered. "How big? I've got a fifteen passenger job from a tour group, seized in a tax deal."

"I was thinking something more in the utility line."

"County Water? It's a theft recovery—the ignition's punched out, but it runs fine."

"Perfect." Russwin smiled at her.

She smiled back, a conspiratorial gleam in her eye. "Now. What else?"

"I need some big guns. Militia stuff, you know. Aryan Nation."

Ace's grin got bigger. "I can hook you up. Stuff I've been saving. I'm drowning in AK's here—meth is a hell of a drug, you know?"

Russwin scrubbed the side of his face with his hand. "Actually . . . I was hoping for something bigger."

That earned him a raised eyebrow. I noticed that it was pierced with a small silver ring. "Bigger?"

"Anti-tank?"

A frown. "Anti-tank? What the hell for?"

Russwin spread his hands. "Hey, if you can't do it, no problem. I was just asking."

"Wait, I didn't say I couldn't do it." She sat back and stared at one of the movie posters, considering.

Russwin waited.

"Am I going to read about this in the *National Enquirer*?"

Russwin shook his head. "Probably not."

Ace switched her attention to me. "How do you figure in this?"

Me? I shrugged. "I just do what people tell me."

She stared at me. I stared back at her. She sighed and looked at Russwin. "If this is a sting, I will lay on you the biggest voodoo curse ever cast. I mean it. Spiders will start crawling out of your ears."

Russwin leaned forward. "Ace, I will go to Leavenworth for life before I roll over on you. You know that."

"Yeah," she said slowly. She seemed to come to a decision.

"I got some TOWs. A half dozen, in crates, launchers, primers, all that shit. Never been opened, far as I can tell. Some grunt at Jefferson Barracks tried to sell them to an FBI plant. The ACLU got involved and the kid got out with a dishonorable discharge. Nobody's ever asked about the gear, but if they do, it's gonna be my ass."

"If it comes to that, call me. I'll take the rap," Russwin said very seriously.

Ace reached into a desk drawer and pulled out a big ring of keys. "Okay, let's get you loaded up before I come to my senses."

The van turned out to be a little bigger than the Quality Electric one, but I felt comfortable backing it down the aisle of lost emergency vehicles until I reached a row of big metal shipping containers. Ace sorted through her keys, muttering, "This never happened."

There were four crates, each the size of a footlocker and heavy enough that I asked Catskinner to help me move them. Ace watched me lift them, amused.

"So that's what he's on loan for."

I glanced back at her. "I also type," I said, and she laughed. It felt good, making her laugh. She was cute, in a post-apocalyptic princess sort of way.

"I'll take a couple of AK's, too, and all the ammo you can give me." Russwin said to Ace, then looked at me. "You want anything for your friend?"

Do you want weapons?

time and space and the spaces between.

"Uh, you got any knives?" I asked Ace.

"Oh, yeah," Ace said expansively, "knives, swords, axes, chainsaws—you should see some of the shit they take off guys in county lockup."

"Let's see," Russwin suggested.

Ace locked up the first shipping container and opened another one. "AK's over there, knives over here."

Take what you want, I told Catskinner.

Unlike the neat lockers and sealed envelopes on CSI, the things that Ace had in the shipping container were just stuffed in bins in no order that I could see. A few of them had tags with faded numbers scribbled on them.

I didn't really expect Catskinner to do anything. He'd never expressed much interest in physical objects, and he'd certainly never expressed any interest in personal possessions. In fact, he always seemed to view my desire to own things and take them with me when we were on the move as a liability. He used objects, if they happened to be close at hand, but he'd never shown me any indication that he ever understood the concept of ownership.

I felt him reach to take control and I eased back, taking a moment to urge him to be very careful. I felt him acknowledge that, and when he spoke he was slow and deliberate.

"i may have these?"

If Ace noticed the change she didn't react. "Sure, if anybody was going to come looking for that crap they would have done it long before now."

Catskinner reached my hands into the tub full of knives and I winced inside, but he was moving gently and deliberately. My fingertips stroked the steel and I felt Catskinner's attention and also his intensity. Almost passion, except that passion in human beings is such a physical thing, heart rate, temperature, breathing, all the body's ways of showing emotion. Catskinner's intensity had no physical component. He wasn't "feeling" anything. Instead, his focus narrowed, his awareness contracting upon the box of blades. It was like watching a slow zoom in a movie or the adjustment of a microscope.

"these are intentional things."

My hands stirred the metal objects, sorting through them quickly but almost silently, and came up with four: a bayonet, a small cleaver, a short, homemade looking blade that seemed to have been made by sharpening a screwdriver on a grinder, and survival knife with a serrated edge. He turned to Ace with the four of them balanced on his open hands.

"*i may have these?*" he repeated.

She had taken several steps back and looked uncomfortable. "Sure," she said slowly.

Russwin was glaring at me. Catskinner sank back out of my body.

say thank you to her.

Thank you? Catskinner?

"Uh, thanks," I said, holding the knives awkwardly. I started looking for ways to put them in my pockets.

"James," Russwin said, emphasizing my name, as if to make sure it was really me he was talking to, "why don't you take the van outside. The gate will open when you get to it. I'll be along in a few minutes."

I nodded, still trying to put the blades away, and headed for the van.

What the hell was that all about?

Silence. Catskinner was a bottomless void in my head, a hole in the fabric of the world, cold, dark, silent, and endlessly empty. In short, he was back to his usual self. I did my best to stash the blades he'd selected in my clothes, the survival knife and the screwdriver in my back pocket, the bayonet in my front pocket. The cleaver was a problem. I stuck it on the dashboard. Catskinner still didn't react.

I had left the van running—the ignition was workable, but awkward. I turned on the radio. It was set to classic rock, I left it there, playing softly. Sitting in the van listening to the radio made me think of Godiva. I told myself that Morgan wouldn't hurt her. He wanted me and would use her to get to me. He couldn't do that if he killed her.

After a while I almost believed it.

Russwin's "few minutes" was closer to twenty, but he did come back to the van, coming out a personnel gate I hadn't noticed.

He swung up into the passenger seat, and I looked over at him. "Well?"

"I guess we find a place to coop for a while. You got cash?"

I nodded. "A couple hundred on me." I thought about it. "More at my motel."

"We just need enough for a room." He thought it over. "Maybe across the river."

I pull the van around and headed in what I thought was the right direction. Something occurred to me. "Shit. I had a bunch stashed in my van, too. Can you check for stolen vehicles or something?"

He shrugged. "I can get it on the hot list." He pulled out his phone. "What's the plate number?"

Uh. I frowned. "I think I've got it at the motel, in the stuff I took from the shop."

"You don't know your plate number." Flat, disgusted. He put his phone away. "No point in calling it in—there's a million white cargo vans on the road."

Well, hell, I never claimed to be secret agent material. I headed for the highway and got caught in a massive traffic mess. There was something big going on downtown—a ball game maybe. I sat and watched the taillights ahead of me and wondered if James Bond had days like this. Of course, his cars had rocket launchers to get rid of the guy ahead of him who was trying to make a left hand turn against the light from the right lane.

Speaking of which.

"So . . . why do we need anti-tank weapons?"

Russwin grinned. "For a frontal attack on the Good Earth."

I stared back. "We're going to attack the Good Earth?"

"Hell, no. That'd be suicide."

"But—you just said."

He nodded. "Look, Ace is a great kid, but she gets lonely and she gets bored. I mean, she's stuck in that damned shack all night.

So she talks to people. She talks to people a lot, about a lot of things."

I was starting "So you think she's going to talk about you and me and the . . . stuff."

"I know she will. Before morning she'll tell somebody. The story's just too good not to share—particularly the way your little friend went ga-ga over the knives. She'll tell somebody, and when she does, Morgan will be listening."

"So you wouldn't really use that stuff."

"Hell, yeah, I would," Russwin said emphatically. "I just hope I don't have to. Morgan's got the next move, I'm just making sure he knows I'm prepared to raise. In this game we can't afford to bluff. Turn right here."

I turned and headed away from downtown, down a side street.

"The highway's a mess—we'll just head south on the surface streets. We can find Motel 6 or something down this way."

"Sure."

We drove for a while without talking. The news came on the radio and Russwin turned it up, but there wasn't anything for us. He turned it back down when the DJ returned.

"We've got to do something," I said at last.

"What?" he asked.

"I don't know. Something." I felt so helpless. It wasn't a feeling I liked.

"Look, Tom White was my partner for six years. We've been through shit together that most people can't even imagine. Right now he's out there somewhere with the side of his head smashed in. Believe me, if there was anything I could do, I'd be doing it."

Russwin stared out the window for a moment. "I've thought about shaking down Morgan's contacts, but he's just got too damned many of them. We could spend all night chasing our tails and ending up with nothing. Like I say, he's got the next move. We needed to resupply, we did that. Now we need to rest up so that when he makes his move we're ready for it."

I nodded. I couldn't fault his logic, I just didn't like it.

"I've got Tom, Alice, and Godiva in the system as persons of interest. If they show up on the radar, I'll get a call. Other than that, if there's anything you can think of, I'm all ears. Has your friend got any ideas?"

Do you? I asked in my head.

he is right. rest, prepare, be ready.

"No," I admitted.

"See?" There was a convenience store coming up on the right. "Pull in here, let's stock up on food."

I pulled in.

"Say," Russwin asked, "Does your friend sleep?"

"I don't think so."

"But you need to, right? I mean, if he tries to keep you going without sleep, it'll mess you up. Like the food thing?"

I saw what he was getting at. "Yeah, he can keep my body awake, it's rough on me."

He nodded and looked momentarily sympathetic. "Yeah. I can imagine."

I opened my door. "You coming in?"

"No, I'll stay with the van. I want to make a couple of calls."

I got some plastic wrapped sandwiches and beef jerky, and a handful of candy bars. Russwin drank soda, so I got him a twelve pack. I thought cops were supposed to be coffee drinkers.

At the register I thought about the food I'd bought for the little suite up by the airport. Godiva's new clothes were there, too. I wished that I was there, with her, watching TV and making popcorn in the cheap white plastic microwave. Even more, I wished I could have invited her to my little apartment above Victor's shop. I'd probably never see that place again. I wondered if I'd ever see Godiva again, if, somehow, we could spend time together, lazy afternoons and quiet evenings, in a place where nobody was looking for us.

Goddamn it, I was tired of running.

Chapter Seventeen

"all of the world is either red or black."

Russwin was on the phone, listening and grunting, when I got back to the van. I broke open the twelve pack and handed him a can, he smiled his thanks and went back to frowning at the phone.

"Nothing," he said to me when he hung up.

I nodded and put the van in gear. "Where to?"

He pointed vaguely south. "There's a Holiday Inn Express a couple miles down."

"I guess where I'm staying isn't safe?"

"Too easy to find."

"But don't we want Morgan to find us?"

"We want him to contact us, not kick in the door shooting."

I guess that made sense.

Russwin went in to talk to the clerk when we got a room and I stayed in the van, very aware of the rocket launchers and machine guns in the back—not to mention four mismatched knives.

Odd. I still didn't understand why Catskinner wanted those particular blades. He had seemed almost . . . emotional about them.

Russwin came back and directed me down the row to our unit. I backed into the space without him having to tell me. That much I knew.

The room was a box with two beds, a TV, and a bathroom. I'd spent way too much of my life in rooms like this. Russwin frowned at the beds.

"You got a preference?"

I shrugged and sat on the one by the window. He slipped off his shoes, put his wallet, his gun, and his phone on the bed table next to the other, and flopped down. He stared up at the ceiling.

I kicked off my shoes, started to stretch out, and then I found Catskinner's knives. I pulled them out of my pockets and put on the bed table. Odd, the cleaver was there, too. I didn't recall picking it up.

"So . . . how did you get messed up in all this . . . stuff?" I asked.

He sighed. "It was one of those inter-agency clusterfucks. A cult compound down in Mississippi. Middle of the swamp—miles from anywhere. DEA was coordinating it, which should have been my first clue the op was doomed from the start."

"So you weren't DEA?"

"Me? Hell, no. Postal inspector. I was supposed to be in a nice safe dry sorting facility, kicking back parcels for insufficient postage. But part of the report alleged these guys were sending controlled substances through U.S. mail, and I had field experience. Ten years in the Corps. MP."

A bitter chuckle. "That's why I wanted to work for the Post Office, you know? I figured I paid my dues and they owed me a nice cushy Fed job.

"Anyway, like I say, it was a mess from the get-go. DEA was in the driver's seat, but there was me from Postal, a couple of grunts from the Bureau, some Customs guys, Mississippi state police, some chick from Border Patrol who looked like she just figured out she was on the wrong bus, and the local sheriff who kept wanting to call a press conference. It was about three in the morning, and I'd been on three planes coming in from DC—this place was nowhere. They flew us in on a couple of Coast Guard choppers. The plan was, we show up in the middle of the night, wave some guns and badges around, and then sit around and process prisoners.

"As soon as we touched down the whole thing went to hell. I

don't know what kind of recon DEA thought they had done, but nobody was home in bed. The whole compound was up and having some kind of festival. We could see the light from the bonfires and hear the drumming half a mile away. The smart thing to do at that point would have been to bug out and come back later, but that was out of the question, too much manpower and too many egos involved. So we slogged on through the mud to join the party."

He fell silent then, and I didn't push him. I wasn't sure I wanted to hear the rest of the story. I had a feeling it didn't end with "they all lived happily ever after."

After a minute or two, "There was maybe a hundred of them, about twenty of us. The head nark in charge comes marching out into the clearing with his bullhorn and starts barking orders and the whole place goes stark raving mad. They were naked, most of them, covered with mud and sweat and blood and God knows what else, and they all just rush us with whatever they've got. Some of them had rocks or sticks, but mostly it was teeth and fingernails. I'd never seen anything like it, and I'd spent years in combat zones.

"Our people were freaking out, shooting up the place—that asshole sheriff had a tactical shotgun and just sprayed the thing like a fire hose. Me, I fell back tried not to use my weapon—these were unarmed civilians, no matter what they were acting like, and I could see prison time looming in my future.

"Then I saw the pillars. A dozen of them, maybe, big stones set in a circle like a poor man's Stonehenge. There were people tied to the pillars. What was left of people, anyway. I remember seeing one guy who missing both his legs, just hanging there by his arms, and he was still... moving. Twitching, kind of. There was a girl—a teenager—her legs weren't touching the ground, but her guts were.

"After that, I started shooting."

He got up. Got a soda. Sat back down. Took a long drink. Looked over at me.

"Then the other things showed up. Things that weren't human anymore. Scales and webbed hands and claws like the Creature from the Black Lagoon. They died hard. It took a lot of shots to drop one of them.

"Anyway, when the smoke cleared me and Tom and those damned pillars were the only things left standing."

"Tom?" I asked. "Tom White?"

"Yeah. He was Bureau then. A marine and a combat veteran like me. One thing about jarheads—we know how to hit the deck in a firefight."

"So that's when you became partners?"

"More or less." He shook his head. "After we . . . after we got back to the choppers we had to deal with the fallout. Two dozen federal agents and God knows how many civilians dead on US soil. The damage control started before we landed at the airport. I told my story so many times to so many people. I was sure I was going to be put in a rubber room in Area 51 or something.

"And then it was over. I was put on indefinite administrative furlough—at full pay, mind you—and told not to talk about what happened. It wouldn't have made any difference if I did—the whole thing was erased from the official record. I have no idea what they told those agents' families."

"It was covered up?" I asked.

"Covered up? It was dropped down a bottomless pit. Everything disappeared. Every file, every memo, every e-mail. Travel vouchers, time cards, expense reports, lab results, court documents, anything relating to the case simply ceased to exist.

"A couple of weeks after I was released Tom walked into the coffee shop where I was getting breakfast. He'd been watching me and decided it was safe to talk. We compared notes and, well, we've been working together ever since."

"thank you for telling me this."

That came as a shock. I hadn't noticed him paying attention.

Russwin looked at me for a long moment. "You're welcome," he said at last.

Then he stretched out on the bed again. "I'm going to get some sleep. If you want to watch TV, go ahead. It won't bother me."

He closed his eyes. As far as I could tell he went straight to sleep.

It wasn't that easy for me. I was thinking about Russwin's story. Thinking about Catskinner's reaction to it. I couldn't think of a single time he had ever said thank you to anyone. And now twice in one night.

Why did you say that to Russwin?

you said we need people.

I did. And I still think it's true. Are you trying to make friends?

cobb russwin is a good man.

A good man? That was another phrase I couldn't ever remember Catskinner using. Was he, after all these years, changing?

Or was it me that was changing? Catskinner saw the world through my eyes, both figuratively and literally. Could it be that it was never really him who had kept the rest of humanity at arms length, that I was the anti-social one, and he was just taking his cues from me?

That was an uncomfortable thought. Instead I thought about what Russwin said at the end, about the operation being erased from official records. How would somebody do that? Why would somebody do that? The Why part was easier—obviously the Outsiders didn't want their existence known. But then, why do they care? What could people do if they knew?

Judging from what I'd managed to accomplish, not much.

So why the secrecy? Maybe how was an easier question after all. Did that mean that the US government was controlled by Outsiders? Not all of it, certainly. Maybe not even most of it— just a few key people in the right places.

Still, though, it seemed like a lot of work for no good reason.

Alice had said that the Outsiders had been influencing human events for centuries—why the big charade?

What did they want?

That was the real question.

And why does Keith Morgan want me dead?

I had a feeling the two questions were connected.

Something Russwin had said earlier in the evening came back to me, something about threat assessment being based on potential. I had the potential to be a threat to Morgan, even if I didn't understand how.

In the same way, the Outsiders were threatened by exposure. There was something that would make them vulnerable, if human beings knew what it was.

So maybe they weren't so invincible after all.

What did we actually know about them? Easier to list what we didn't know about them. We don't know where they came from, or how they communicate with humans, or how they do any of the things they could do.

We know that they lie. What did Alice say? They claim to be whatever people will listen to; angels, demons, aliens, dead relatives, spirit guides. . . .

They don't want most of the human race to know they exist. They used people, but they lied to them. Whatever they were, they kept it secret.

Which meant they lied to Keith Morgan, too. That was something to keep in mind.

Russwin's phone woke me, which made me realize that I had fallen asleep.

He was awake in an instant, opening his eyes and rolling over and answering the phone all in one motion while I was still struggling with figuring out where I was.

I had the feeling that I had thought of something important, something that I should remember, but I lost it. Russwin was slipping into his shoes while he talked.

"Yes, I know Tom White. He's my partner."

A long sigh.

"What's his condition?"

"I understand. I'm on my way."

"Wait—you do understand that he's a federal agent involved in an ongoing investigation, right? Is there any way you can get some security on his room?"

"Perfect. Thank you so much. Also, be advised that his only living relative is his mother, and she's in a nursing home in San Diego. If anyone claims to be a relative, stall them, okay?"

He looked around the room, looked at me. "I dunno, maybe a half hour? As quick as I can."

"Thank you again."

He hung up the phone, slid his gun into his holster.

I'd found one of my shoes by then.

"Was that about White?" I asked, just to show I'd been paying attention.

"He is Christian Northeast. ICU."

"Give me a second." There was my other shoe.

Russwin grabbed a soda. I could feel his impatience.

Once I had my shoes on Catskinner took my arms and grabbed his knives, then moved me to the door.

"*you drive.*" he told Russwin.

Russwin paused to grab the twelve pack of soda and stuff the wrapped sandwiches in it. He handed it to me, Catskinner took it.

On the way out the door Russwin asked, "Can you eat? Or does James have to do that?"

Catskinner seemed to be confused by the question. I answered for him, and took my body back at the same time.

"He doesn't understand how food works. It's tough to explain." I swung up into the passenger seat of the van, put the soda and sandwiches at my feet.

Russwin got in the driver's seat, looking thoughtful.

The streets were empty and Russwin took them just a little faster than he should have, then put his foot to the floor once we got on the highway. Of course, we were in a Water Company van, top speed wasn't much over the speed limit. Still, we were at the hospital in less than the half hour he'd estimated.

It took us another twenty minutes to get to White's room. Russwin went over the security arrangements with the front desk, showing his ID and introducing himself to the staff. I trailed along behind him, he introduced me as a confidential informant to anyone who asked, but most people didn't.

He *was* a good man, I realized. Confident and controlled. He understood how things worked, the bureaucracy of the hospital and how to talk to the uniformed officers in front of White's door. He would be a good ally.

They let us go into the room by ourselves. Tom White lay in the bed with the usual tubes and wires and machines. He wasn't on a respirator, which I figured was a good sign. The side of his head was wrapped up, but other than that he looked like he was just asleep.

Chapter Eighteen

"the night is the day's winter."

Russwin went and sat beside the hospital bed. I stood by the door.

"How are you doing, buddy?" Russwin said quietly. "You don't look so good. I don't know if you can hear me, but I got the son of a bitch that did this. I put a pair of county cops on the door, too. You just rest up and get better, you hear me? You'll be okay."

He reached out and touched White's hand. "I got a message for you, too. We saw Ace, picked up some stuff. She said—and I quote—tell him that I want to live in his heart forever, but I'll settle for getting in his pants tonight."

Russwin laughed. "I don't know how you do it, buddy. She's got it bad for you."

He sat quietly for a while. I stood by the door and looked at my feet.

"You get better now, you hear me?" Russwin was almost whispering. "This shit's getting ugly. This is not the time to be lying down on the job."

He scrubbed his face with his hand. "What the hell time is it, anyway?"

I found a clock on one of the machines. "Almost four," I said.

"See if you can find a doctor, okay?"

I nodded and went out. One of the uniformed officers was sitting on a folding chair by the door, the other one was empty.

156

The cop looked up at me. "What's the story, anyway?"

I shrugged. "I don't know much. I'm . . . uh, DEA. On loan from the Tucson office." I used to live in Tucson so I figured the DEA had an office there, and if they didn't they should.

"Drugs, huh." The cop nodded just as if I'd explained something. "Bad news, a cop getting hurt like that."

"Yeah. Say, do you know where I could find a doctor?"

He pointed down the hall. "Try the nurses station."

"Thanks." It took me a good half hour of aimless wandering before I found a middle-aged man who was willing to admit that he was the doctor assigned to Tom White. Hospitals in the middle of the night have a unique emptiness, they seemed to be designed to be empty like some airless city on the moon where anything living is unwelcome.

Then again, I'm prejudiced. I spent my childhood in locked wards. I still have nightmares in which I hear the sound of footsteps echoing on tile.

Anyway, I got back to the room with the doctor. Russwin was sitting by White's bed. He got up, introduced himself, and shook hands with the doctor.

"What can you tell me?" Russwin asked.

The doctor looked at the chart. "Agent White was brought in about nine last evening. An anonymous 911 call reported a man unresponsive in the parking lot of the QT gas station about a mile from here. Paramedics found him lying on the ground beside the pay phone where the call was made. His wounds were dressed, a very good field dressing, actually, looks like it was made from the victim's shirt.

"He suffered a severe skull fracture. We were able to remove the skull fragments and relieve the pressure on his brain, but at this point there is no way to tell what long-term effects he may face. Six months from now he may be completely recovered—"

"—or he might never wake up," Russwin finished for him.

The doctor frowned. "There's still too much we simply don't know about brain injuries. I will say that he is breathing on his own, uh," he looked at his watch, "about five hours after surgery. In my experience that's a positive sign."

"Thank you, doctor." Russwin looked over at White. "Two tours in the Gulf without a scratch on him, and then this happens in the States."

"The wound has a very unusual shape—is there anything you can tell me about how it happened?"

"No, I wasn't there. Did he have anything with him when he was picked up?"

The doctor paged through the chart. "Just his clothing. No personal effects. It evidently took a while to ID him through fingerprints. At first the FBI said he wasn't on file, then they called back and gave you as the point of contact."

"He's detached from the Bureau. We're on special assignment through the State department."

"The admissions desk said you had some information regarding Agent White's next of kin?"

"Yes, his mother's name is Joan White, and she lives in San Diego, she's in a nursing home—I can't remember the specifics, but I can get that information to you over the next couple of days. She's, uh, pretty confused these days. A couple of years ago Tom set up a trust fund for her care, when he moved her into the home. To be honest, I don't know if she's responsible enough to make, uh, any decisions regarding . . . you know."

The doctor nodded gravely. "Well, we'll keep you informed of his status."

Russwin gave him a card. "Please do. That's my cell phone, and also an office in DC where you can leave messages if I don't pick up."

The doctor glanced at me. During the whole exchange I had been trying to pretend I wasn't there, so I just nodded. He turned back to Russwin.

"I'm sorry, but I really can't give you anything more at this time. We've done what we can. Now it's just a matter of waiting to see how things develop. How he weathers the next few days will tell us more. Right now there are just too many unknown factors to make any predictions."

"I understand." Russwin took a last look at the still figure on the bed, then headed for the door. "Please, call me when there's something to report."

I opened the door for him and we headed out. Both cops were at the door now, he paused and said, "I don't think you men are going to have any trouble, but I'm glad you're here just in case. Some of these Ukrainians are just flat out psycho."

The cops nodded their agreement. The one I'd spoken to before said, "We'll keep our eyes open."

We didn't talk on our way back out of the ICU. There didn't seem to be anything to say. Aside from a thin woman in a white uniform slow dancing with a floor buffer, we didn't see a living thing on the way out.

There was a blue sheet of paper stuck under the van's windshield wiper. I pulled it free. A flier, advertising something called the Seventh Midwestern SETI/Encounter Convention. A UFO convention, it looked like. I started to pitch it.

"Wait, give me that," Russwin said.

I handed it to him and got in the driver's seat. Russwin got in more slowly, studying the flier.

He held it out to me. "Read the last line."

The last line was in large type and bold.

the Great misunderstanding of Our time is the iDea that we are alone In the uniVerse and we Are not!

The capitalization was screwy, but I kind of expected that. . .

Wait a second...

G.-O-D-I-V-A. Godiva.

I looked at the information. The convention was being held at a banquet hall in South County and the opening ceremonies were tomorrow at three in the afternoon. Well, technically, today at three in the afternoon.

I looked over at Russwin "This is—?"

"Morgan's move. Yeah." He sighed.

"So, what do we do?"

"We show up and try not to get killed. But first we get some sleep."

Try not to get killed and get some sleep. Great. He was starting to sound like Catskinner.

"Can't we . . . I don't know . . . do some research? Case the joint or something?"

Russwin rubbed his temples. "We've got about ten hours. That's not enough to find out anything useful. Ordinarily I'd call Alice and ask her if she had any intel on this group, but that's not an option right now, is it?"

Alice. Morgan had her, too. I'd forgotten about that.

"I guess." I backed the van out of the space. I remembered how we got here, so I could get back to the motel.

"Look." Long sigh. "It's a trap. We know it's a trap. They know that we know it's a trap. We know that they know, et fucking cetera. We can walk into it, or we can run away. I'm not running."

I thought about it. I was good at running. I'd spent my whole life doing it. But . . . not this time. Not when things were maybe going to change for me. I couldn't go back.

But it wasn't just me.

we won't run.

I could die, you know. This could kill me, and then you'd have nowhere to go.

we won't run.

"Me, either."

"Then let's get some sleep."

I pulled onto the highway. "What I don't understand is—is this whole convention just for our benefit?"

"Huh? No, it's probably been in the works for months. Just another group that Morgan has his fingers on."

"But Godiva's name in the flier?"

"Oh, that? That's a new flier, printed out special for us."

I considered. "So . . . Morgan had to find us, get hold of someone to add a new line to the flier, and come out and put it on our van in the middle of the night?"

"Yep."

"That's a lot of work. Couldn't he have just called you?"

"Sure. But that wouldn't have sent the same message."

"What message?"

"He wants us to know that he's got this UFO cult in his pocket. He's trying to intimidate us."

"Oh. Is it working?"

"Pretty much. We're fucked. You do know that, right?"

I sighed. "Yeah, I figured that part out."

I drove south. The sunrise was red over the river at my right hand.

At one o'clock in the afternoon we were eating lunch at a pancake house. I insisted. If we were going to die, I refused to have my last meal handed to me through a drive-thru window. We'd slept, showered, and in Russwin's case, shaved. Me, I didn't care what I looked like.

Russwin nursed a soda and watched me engulf an order of chicken fried steak and eggs, plus pancakes.

"Not much puts you off your feed, does it?" he asked, amused.

I shrugged. "I'm always hungry—always have been."

A considering look. "I guess that makes sense—you're eating for two."

"Yeah. And one of them isn't human." I was finished. I pushed my plate away and dropped cash on the table. "Let's go."

Russwin stood up. "Right. We want to make sure we get good seats."

The woman at the registration desk was wearing a T-shirt with my father's picture on it. I'm sure she thought I was staring at her tits—which, to be honest, were worth a second look—but she looked down, looked back at me and said, "Michael Chase. A true visionary."

I looked away. "I know exactly who he was." Russwin paid for two admissions, collected two badges. He hung one around my neck and Catskinner let him. I grabbed a program off the stack and looked at it.

Well, let's see. There was a panel discussion on something called "Bell's Conjecture" that started at 4:00, and the ever popular "George Adamski: Notes And Observations" forum at 5:15—no information on who George Adamski is or why I should care about him—and then an EXCLUSIVE (with lots of exclamation marks) advance screening of *We Pass From View*—

—wait a second. *We Pass From View*? Somebody made a movie of one of my father's books? And that one? There wasn't any story there. I pointed that out to Russwin as we walked away from the registration desk.

"I don't get it. It's not like there are any characters. It's just a bunch of theories. I mean, do they just have some guy saying, 'This is what some people think happens when you die, and this is what other think happens when you die, and this is what I think happens when you die.' It's got to be the dumbest movie ever."

He sighed. "Just be quiet, okay?"

"Seriously, it's like making a movie of, I don't know, *Windows For Dummies* or something—"

Quietly, but very forcefully: "Shut. Up."

That got my attention. I looked up from the program.

We had acquired an escort. Two men, one big guy, about Russwin's size, with tattoos covering his arms and a bushy biker beard. The other was huge, about seven feet tall, with that gaunt Abe Lincoln look that so many really big men have. They were watching us and making no attempt to conceal it. If the intent was to be intimidating it didn't quite work. Catskinner isn't impressed with size. Giants have weak joints.

I stuffed the program in my pocket and looked around. Everybody except for us and our big shadows seemed to have someplace to go and most of them were late, judging from the rush.

There was a Meeting Room A, and a Meeting Room B. One of them was having that panel about what's-his-name's thingie, and the other one was having the talk about that other guy I couldn't remember.

Then there was Screening Room—where the movie version of *We Pass From View* was going to have its Exclusive!! Premier!! later on in the evening. Right now something else was playing in there—dark room, probably crowded, limited mobility, no, not a good option.

That left the Vendor's Room. Perfect. Maybe we could buy some moon rocks or pixie dust or something. I met Russwin's eye and nodded towards it. He fell into step beside me.

There was a bored security guard in a gray uniform sitting by the door. Inside the room tables were set up on both long sides, maybe twenty in all. Behind the tables were the sellers. Milling around in a mass in the middle of the room were the buyers, on the tables was the stuff.

Books, a lot of books. But also DVD's, magazines, T-shirts, a table loaded down with crystals, another one with a selection of knives—

—You want a knife?

i have enough for now, thank you—

—one that was full of tiny bottles of God knows what, one

set up with a row of laptop computers that people were entering information into.

Russwin and I wandered around, trying to look at everything without getting close enough to any particular table to trigger a sales pitch. So was everyone else, so in a way we were blending in. Except for being followed by a pair of thugs, of course.

Catskinner didn't like the crowd. He wasn't particularly concerned about our shadows; it was the whole roomful of people, moving, talking wandering in the usual chaotic social Brownian motion of human beings everywhere and getting too close for comfort. I could feel Catskinner's awareness flitting from person to person and I was acutely conscious of the mismatched blades tucked in my clothes. This could get ugly.

By reflex I moved to the edge of the room, Russwin staying close without looking like it was intentional, the biker and the giant simply stalking the pair of us without apology. I moved to the end of the row of tables, trying to get most of the crowd on one side of me so Catskinner could keep my eyes on them without breaking my neck.

The last table was the one with the laptops on it. "Repressed Memory Testing" the signs said. How do you test a repressed memory? Play Concentration with a blindfold? I glanced at Russwin. He seemed to be utterly fascinated with the table across the hall, which had stacks of old magazines wrapped in individual plastic bags.

What the hell were we even doing here?

you are looking for godiva. i am hunting keith morgan. he is avenging his partner.

And how does shopping for UFO cult crap do any of that?

No answer. Naturally.

So what else could I do? Grab those two that had been watching us and torture them for information? Well, why not? Obviously somebody told them to watch us, so somebody knows something.

Besides, the biker one kept giving me this tough guy glare and after the last few days I wouldn't mind watching Catskinner peel it off his skull. I wouldn't mind at all.

Then the person next to me turned and walked away from the table and I realized that I had joined the line waiting to take the test on a laptop without realizing it. It was my turn, if I wanted to take it.

Russwin was talking to the woman who ran the used magazine table. What the hell. I turned and looked at the screen.

This test—the screen informed me—was developed by the Air Force as part of the debriefing of pilots who exhibited erratic behavior following long term high altitude flight. The questions were written by military psychologists who were experts in the field of post-traumatic stress and memory repression and is 97% effective in uncovering evidence of close encounters that have been unconsciously repressed by the respondents.

Fascinating. I clicked past that part.

<u>Do you ever find yourself doing things without fully under-standing the reason why?</u>

Brother, you have no idea.

I have taken a couple of hundred psychological profile tests in my time, and I knew what answers meant what and how to get whatever score I wanted. I was going to play with it and get it to say that I had definitely been abducted by aliens and probably impregnated by them, but at the second question Catskinner reached out and closed the lid of the laptop—gently, it didn't shatter.

I hadn't even got to tell it which animal I'd rather be. Instead I found myself face to face with one of the men who ran this table. The man was about forty, I guessed, with long brown hair streaked with gray and a small neatly trimmed beard. His eyes were absolutely empty. Holes in the world, leading the the darkness between the stars.

I'd seen those eyes before, catching a glimpse of my own face in a mirror when Catskinner was riding me. Catskinner and whatever was looking out through that man's face stared at each other for a long moment. Something passed between them—greeting, challenge, question and answer, I had no way of knowing—and then I was turning away. Russwin was at my elbow.

"Are you okay?"

"Yeah, sure," I said. I fumbled the program out of my pocket. "I think they said there was a bar in this place somewhere?"

Russwin nodded, headed to the door. I followed. The biker and the giant fell into step behind me.

What the hell was that?

nothing.

Friend of yours?

nothing.

Chapter Nineteen

"the enemy of my enemy is the enemy of my enemy, nothing more."

I studied the map on the program. It didn't even try to be to scale. Here was the vendor's room— Meeting Room B—so the Hospitality Suite should be . . . there. Or maybe the other way. I wasn't good with maps. I looked up to get my bearings, and there was the biker, giving me his tough guy glare from across the corridor, the giant standing behind him.

"Hey, buddy," I called across to them. Russwin, a few steps down the hallway, stopped and looked back, his hand going inside his jacket reflexively.

A frown replaced the glare. I was breaking thug etiquette. I was supposed to pretend I didn't notice them or something.

"So where's the bar?" I gave him a grin. "I'm kind of lost."

He looked confused, then pointed down the hall the way Russwin had been headed.

"Thanks," I turned my back on them. Russwin gave me a sharp look, then grinned, visibly relaxing.

A thought occurred to me, and I glanced back at our escort.

Ask him something, I thought to Catskinner. Ask him if you can buy him a drink.

"can i buy you a drink?"

Both men reacted, recoiled slightly at Catskinner's voice. I saw surprise and confusion and just a hint of fear.

"I don't drink," the biker said stiffly, his eyes wary.

I turned back and head down the hall. They weren't expecting Catskinner, no one had prepped them on what I am. Interesting. Russwin didn't react, but I was sure he'd picked up on it, too.

Past Room A and Room B and the Screening Room and something called Convention Services (and the omnipresent Men's and Ladies') was a room called Hospitality. The door was open. Inside a bar was set up along one wall with a bartender in a black suit. A couple of steam tables were set up along the other wall, but they were empty and dry.

A dozen or so people stood around with plastic cups in their hands. They were more of the same that had been in the vender's room—serious young people in T-shirts that were meant to be shocking but were mostly just silly, the men with beards, the women with brightly dyed hair, all of them looking vaguely unwell.

We passed through pockets of conversation on the way to the bar, most of them concerned with who else was here and what had happened in their lives since the last convention. We were the focus of attention and not just from our shadows, who took up station near the door. I assumed it was Russwin—he couldn't be anything other than a cop of some kind, and this seemed to be a crowd who took conspiracy theories seriously.

Of course, Russwin really *was* a federal agent who worked outside of the ordinary chain of command in order to conceal evidence of alien activity, so maybe they were on to something after all.

We ordered sodas at the bar. I asked for some whiskey in mine. As far as I could tell, alcohol had no effect on Catskinner's functioning at all and I needed to relax.

No one was actually sitting at the bar, so we took the two stools in the middle. Convention attendees came and went, getting drinks, drinking them, and leaving again. A sign at the door said that alcoholic beverages couldn't be taken from the room, but nobody wanted to miss anything by hanging out longer than it took to slug back a cup of booze.

"What are we doing here?" I asked.

"Waiting," Russwin said simply.

"Waiting for what?"

"For them to stop playing games and offer us a deal."

"*i won't accept it.*"

Russwin raised his eyebrows at Catskinner's words. "Let's hear what it is first."

"He didn't accept the last deal Morgan offered," I pointed out. I was getting used to Catskinner injecting himself into conversations.

"Yeah, but that was before you took out the minraudim and the tin man. Your bargaining position is better now."

And Morgan had Godiva, and Alice, which meant his bargaining position was better, too. At least with me, but he didn't really want to make a deal with me. Hostages wouldn't make any difference to Catskinner. He hadn't changed that much.

Russwin turned to look back so I looked, too. Our shadows were talking to someone.

She was all in red. Polished boots with spike heels, stockings, short skirt, tight blouse, even her hair was a uniform shade of bright red. I wondered if she was one of those ambimorphs—her body was good enough. She looked over at the pair of us and smiled, and her lips were the same shade. In contrast her skin seemed pale, washed out. She walked to the bar, smiling, striding confidently.

The negotiator had arrived at last.

She spoke when she was still a few feet away, heading for the chair next to me. "Most of the people in the building are completely innocent."

It seemed an odd thing to say. Catskinner answered her, "*that means nothing to me.*"

"True," she agreed, sliding into the chair beside me, "but it means something to Adam."

"My name is James," I told her pointedly, "and I think you overestimate my concern for innocent bystanders."

"James," she said, "that's right. I'd forgotten. I'm Agony Delapour." She looks past me, "And this must be Corbett Russwin."

"Charmed," Russwin said. "Agony, huh? Cute name."

"It is, isn't it?" She smiled. Her teeth, like her skin, seemed unnaturally white. I wondered if they were false, like Godiva's.

"So, you're here to offer us Morgan's terms?"

That earned a laugh. "Oh, heavens, no!" She gestured to the bartender. "Mike, if you would?"

The bartender nodded, opened a small fridge below the bar, and brought out a white bucket. He lifted it up so that we could see into it without showing it to the crowd who still mingled aimlessly behind us.

In the bucket was a human head, with ice packed around it. Keith Morgan's head. Frozen blood rimed the stump of his neck.

Well. I wasn't expecting that.

I drained my drink, set the empty cup on the bar.

"Gimme another. No ice."

Another laugh from Agony.

Russwin sighed deeply, but when he spoke his voice was calm. "What do you want?"

"From you? Nothing. You're not really a threat, and I don't see how you could be useful." She looked back at me. "You, on the other hand, are a very useful threat."

"I'm sorry, but I don't think Catskinner's going to deal with you. He wouldn't take the contract that Morgan offered him."

"Covenant," Agony corrected me. "And Morgan was very foolish, which is why he's a head in bucket now. He underestimated what you are."

"Okay, then, you've got Godiva and Alice. How about you let them go and I leave you alone?"

"Perhaps I don't want you to leave me alone."

I sighed. "What? You want me to kill somebody for you? It's all I'm good at."

"You also underestimate yourself." She stood. "Enjoy the convention."

"Wait!" I stood, face to face with her. In her heels she was as tall as me. "Where are they?"

"Oh, they're around here someplace." She waved her hand at the rest of the convention center. "If you touch me you'll never see them again, of course."

I stepped back. "I'm tired and I really don't have any patience for this shit. Tell me what you want."

She leaned forward and said softly, "I just want you to be happy, Adam."

Then she turned and walked away. I stood there and watched her go. I didn't know what else I could do.

Beside me Russwin stood. "We better do what she said."

"What do you mean?"

"Enjoy the convention. Godiva and Alice are around here someplace."

Agony had left, leaving most of the crowd staring after her. Not our shadows, though, the biker and the giant were back to watching us.

I reached for my drink, finished it, set it back down. "Okay, let's look around."

I pulled the program out of my pocket. The Adamski panel was still going on, but in Room A the Bell's Conjecture discussion would have ended, and something called "Suppressed Evidence: A Slide Show" was starting in a few minutes. In the Screening Room *Chariots of the Gods* was about half over.

"Where do you want to start?"

Russwin looked over my shoulder. "Suppressed Evidence," he said. "It's what's starting next."

We headed down the hall and our shadows followed.

Chapter Twenty

"welcome to the butcher's hour."

I expected the thugs to follow us, but I wasn't expecting them to step up to the table in the front of the room. There was a laptop set up, cables snaking back to a projector on a rolling cart in the aisle between the ranks of folding chairs. The biker fiddled with it, frowning at the screen. The giant stood silently behind him, watching us.

There were a score of conventioneers scattered randomly throughout the room, most of them standing and talking. One stood by herself in the corner of the room. She looked familiar—

"Alice", Russwin said softly. He crossed the room quickly, I followed. Alice brightened to see us.

"Oh, thank God, Cobb—I'm so sorry about Tom—they were waiting in the parking lot—" She was near panic. Russwin put his arm around her.

"Tom's at Christian Northeast," he said quietly. "The doctor said he's got a chance to recover. We just have to wait and see."

Alice breathed a sigh that seemed to deflate her. "They did drop him off. I didn't think they would." She switched her attention to me. "Godiva's here. I don't know where. They separated us, told me to wait here."

"Who's they?" I asked.

She shook her head. "I don't know. They act like nestlings, but I don't think they're local. I guess Morgan brought in some out of town muscle."

"Not Morgan," Russwin said.

"Morgan's dead," I said. "We just saw his head in an ice chest."

Alice gasped and Russwin glared at me. "Sorry," I said. I guess Alice didn't really need all the details.

She recovered nicely, though. "But . . . what the fuck?"

"There's a new player. Calls herself Agony Delapour. She evidently took out Morgan. I guess she's taking over his empire."

Alice shook her head. "Don't know her."

"Excuse me." Even amplified the biker's voice was surprisingly hesitant. "We're kind of on a schedule here, so if everyone could just take their seats..."

I looked around and saw that was mostly directed at us, since just about everyone else was seated.

We moved to take the nearest folding chairs under the disapproving scowls of the conventioneers.

"Thank you."

They'd set up a projection screen at the front of the room. Oh, yeah, this was going to be a slide show. "Do we have to stay for this?" I asked Russwin in a whisper.

"Delapour wants us to see this for a reason. Until we know what that is, yes."

"Now, uh," the biker's voice over the PA was at odds with his grizzled appearance. He sounded like the ninety-pound weakling from the old Charles Atlas ads. "Could someone get the lights, please?"

Someone got up and the lights went out. The projector illuminated the room with a blue screen and the words "No Signal" across the screen.

"Now, just hang on a second," the biker said, mostly to himself. He fiddled with the laptop connections and the screen lit up with a shot of the laptop desktop. The wallpaper was a blurry snapshot of a kitten and a German shepherd sharing a wicker chair on somebody's sun porch.

Quite the professional presentation. I chuckled and voices out of the darkness shushed me.

He clicked around on the screen and a title card came up. "Evidence Of Extraterrestrial Infiltration" it read.

"Okay, now, what you're about to see is pretty disturbing stuff. It's new—very, very new—and I've only seen the images once myself. Be warned."

The title card was replaced by a picture of Godiva. She was standing in an empty white room dressed in the clothes I'd bought for her, her glasses on, her teeth in place. She was looking at the camera, bright lights casting dark shadows behind her. She looked very scared, and very alone.

I started in my seat, started to get up. Russwin grabbed my arm. "Steady, there, cowboy," he whispered to me. "Let's see where this goes. The more we know, the better."

I settled back, biding my time. I was going to find out what they knew and where she was, and then I was going to go get her.

"Now, uh, this looks like an ordinary person, I mean, a human person, right?"

Murmured assent from the crowd.

The scene changed. The next shot was Godiva's face. A pair of hands held her head. Her glasses were off and her green on green eyes were tearing from the lights. The murmurs became excited. Chairs moved in the dimness as people leaned closer.

"Uh, as you can see, there are some differences, though—"

The scene changed again. Now her teeth had been removed and the hands held her jaw open. Inside her mouth there was a cluster of dark tendrils—the strangeness that I'd glimpsed but never seen directly. Her eyes were closed tightly.

I shut my own. I knew how she felt about the changes that had been wrought to her and I felt her humiliation at being exposed this way.

You will have work to do tonight, I promised Catskinner privately.

wait. soon, he replied.

The scene changed. I stood. Not soon, I told Catskinner. Now.

Godiva was lying on her back, held down by two sets of arms. She was naked and her legs spread wide. The crowd gasped, and there was a buzz of whispered conversation. I didn't care. The show ended now. I walked to the front table. Behind me I heard Russwin saying something, probably urging calm. I wasn't listening.

The biker saw me coming. "Now, just hang on for a few minutes, let me finish. I did say these images were disturbing."

"The show ends now," I said.

The giant moved to block my way. I felt Catskinner focusing, but he held back and let me stay in control of my body. I felt angry enough to tear the giant apart by myself.

"Now, you really have to see this in context," the biker was saying, fumbling with the controls of the laptop.

The next shot showed Godiva on a steel table. She was lying on her back. Something transparent was covering her, something like a cocoon or a chrysalis. I stared, unable to make sense of the image.

"Here we have the creature restrained," the biker was saying, and I realized what I was seeing. It looked like someone had taken a roll of that clear plastic that they used to wrap pallets and wrapped Godiva and the table together, binding her.

"Where is she?" I shouted. I pushed past the giant—not Catskinner, me—and I felt less in control than when he was riding me. The giant grabbed me by the shoulder and only then did I feel Catskinner reach out with my arm and toss him to the ground. The rest of me was still mine.

I heard Russwin hiss, "Stay down, big fellow," and realized he was talking to the giant. I hadn't heard him come up behind me.

"That will become clear," the biker said, "if you would please just—"

"Where. Is. She." I was shaking. Make him tell me, I told Catskinner.

The screen changed again. More layers of plastic had been added, covering her face, obscuring the contours of her body. A slit was cut down the center of her form, through the plastic, through her skin and muscle, exposing her internal organs.

Dead. They had killed her. And then they had dissected her. I had seen death before. I had seen atrocities preformed by my own hands. Maybe I deserved this. Maybe the relatives of Catskinner's victims felt like this. I closed my eyes. I didn't care.

New plan, I said in my head. He dies. His big friend dies. Everybody in this damned place dies. Now.

Catskinner opened my eyes. My hands were already reaching for his knives. The biker started to say something and my hand lashed out with the modified screwdriver and thrust it into his neck until it grated against his spinal cord. The physical symptoms of the rage were gone, replaced by the cold distance of my body, but I still felt the need to do something, to react, and if I couldn't erase the fact of Godiva's murder I could damned sure erase the ones responsible.

"James—wait!" I heard Alice shouting. Neither Catskinner nor I reacted. We had business to take care of. My body started to turn. For once I felt unified with Catskinner, I understood him. I could see humans the way he say them, through his mind looking through my eyes and seeing chaos, walking filth, noise that cried out to be silenced. This wasn't murder, this was curing cancer.

Then Russwin came out of the darkness and bowled me over. Catskinner rolled with the impact and Russwin kept going, into the corner of the table and knocking it over. My feet were back under me and I was turning, facing the giant in the dim light reflected from the slide on the screen. There was steel in both my hands, and everything was in motion.

The giant was facing me. He had gotten bigger. He had also grown scales, and claws, and big teeth and a tail. Okay. Not human.

Did you know he could do that?

their contraplicate nature was obscured.

The lizardman hissed and swung a fistful of claws at my face—fast. Catskinner dodged out of the way. My hands lashed out with both knives and he dodged. Not good.

Catskinner swung the table around and it got tangled up in the lizardman's legs (the screen going back to the No Signal blue as the laptop went clattering off someplace) and he went down, which was good, but he was able to roll out of the path of Catskinner's descending knives and lash out with a foot—also clawed—which Catskinner dodged by leaping straight up in the air and coming down with both feet on the lizardman's tail, which must have hurt because I could feel little bones splintering, but he was striking back, curled in a tighter curve than a human could have managed and biting, ripping my pants but—I hoped—not my skin.

All of which happened before Russwin could get up. The other audience members hadn't even begun to react. Somewhere in the darkness behind the lizardman was Alice. I hoped that she'd be able to get clear.

Then we were back at it, slash, dodge, jump, slash, roll, neither the lizardman's claws or Catskinner's knives able to connect. Catskinner had never fought anyone as fast as he was before. I didn't know how long he could keep it up before burning up all my reserves, but I knew it couldn't be long.

At some point we knocked the screen down and the beam of the projector cast a fuzzy blue glow across the walls and ceiling. Out of the corner of my eye I caught the biker's body and it looked strange, deformed somehow, but Catskinner's attention was focused on the lizardman.

"Duck!" Russwin yelled and my body hit the ground. Russwin fired—the same steady rhythm as when he was shooting at the minraudim, one and two and three and four and five. The lizardman was moving, down and around and tying to make for Russwin, but I think he was hit three times, maybe four. It staggered him, slowed him down enough that Catskinner was able to jackknife up and bury the bayonet in one reptilian eye and the screwdriver in the other. Blood, pale pink and watery, sheeted his scaly hide.

Make sure it's dead, I suggested.

of course.

My hand left the bayonet in place and returned with the cleaver. Holding the lizardman's body upright with the screwdriver Catskinner chopped, after three swings the body fell, leaving me holding the head.

it's dead.

I took my body and Catskinner let me. I was instantly weak. It wasn't just the usual hunger; I was bone weary. Human bodies weren't designed to operate at Catskinner's level, it was like hooking a 110 volt motor to a 220 line. It worked great for short bursts, but my body needed time to recover. Over the last few days Catskinner had taken my body more often than in the previous month, and the strain was showing more and more. I didn't know how close my nervous system was to burning out, and I didn't think Catskinner did either.

Russwin came up beside me.

"Sic transit tyrannosaurus," he said softly, looking down at the body of the lizardman. I realized I was still holding the head, so I dropped it.

the others still live.

Let them. I don't care about them. I didn't care about much of anything. I was exhausted, body and soul. Godiva was dead, Morgan was dead. I didn't have anywhere to go or anything to do, except leave here.

they seem to care about you.

I looked out at the crowd. Some of them were out of their chairs, some heading to exits, some on the floor, all of them staring at us. Yeah, heck of a show, huh?

Beside me I heard Russwin reloading his pistol. I didn't know where Alice was.

"We'll, uh, we'll just be leaving now," I said.

my knives.

Right. I reached down and pulled the screwdriver loose from the lizardman's head. The bayonet was a little trickier, I had to put my foot on the head to hold it in place and yank. It came free and I utterly failed to conceal how shaky I was on my feet. Not good, I wanted to crowd to still be scared of me, at least long enough to reach the exit.

"Cobb!" Alice called from someplace behind us. "We have a problem."

Russwin turned to look, his head and his gun swiveling together like synchronized swimmers. He looked back to me, then at the assembled crowd.

"Ladies and gentleman, you need to leave this room at once. Please, everybody, gather your belongings, and if somebody could get the lights, please." His voice was calm, commanding, a perfect cop voice.

It worked, too, for a moment. Then the first people to reach the doors pushed on them and they didn't open. Then the people behind them started pushing. And still no one got the lights.

I turned to look at whatever it was that Alice and Russwin had seen. My eyes had adjusted pretty well to the blue light from the projector. On the floor by my feet was the lizardman's body, and the lizardman's head, and over there was the biker's body, or, rather, the biker's bones. Bones? The bones gleamed wetly in the blue light and there was some kind of pool of liquid, like the one around Victor's body, but it was in the wrong place, it was closer to me than the bones.

And it was moving. Toward me. I stepped back and Russwin reached out, guided me around him to the other side of him. The fluid didn't change direction as I half expected it to, it kept rolling across the floor until it reached the lizardman's body. The lizardman started liquefying, the inhuman bones poking through the flesh and the pool growing, spreading. It was thicker than blood. In the blue light it looked like yogurt.

"What's that?" I asked Russwin. I really didn't want to know, it was just habit.

"Can somebody please get the lights on?" Russwin's voice was starting to lose its calm control, but a moment later the lights came on, dazzling us all. In the light from the overheads the pool of goo was pink. A pale pink, the color of lips.

Russwin headed to one of the doors, his gun held loosely, pointed at the floor. Alice joined us quickly. As we reached the people struggling to push the door Russwin said loudly, "Stand aside—let's get us all out of here."

They weren't panicked, not quite or not yet, so they parted grudgingly to let us through. It was a simple set of double doors, with commercial panic bars. I pushed on the door, and it depressed, but the door didn't open. Something was holding it closed from the other side.

"I tried that," a man said angrily.

"They're not supposed to lock those," another man added. "Fire codes."

I pushed harder, and the door didn't budge. I didn't like it, but I was going to have to ask Catskinner to come out, one more time.

Then the screaming started. Someone at the edge of the crowd had fallen, but he wasn't the one screaming. He was melting into pink goo—the ones around him were screaming.

We need out of here now.

In answer Catskinner threw my body against the door, hard enough to bend the door and crack the paint, but it still didn't open. He moved back for another run and Alice yelled, "The wall! Go through the wall!"

Catskinner changed my direction and brushed a couple in matching T-shirts out of the way and hit the wall. Drywall caved and a stud splintered and then I was through, out into the hallway. I saw a frame of 2x4's nailed up over the door, and then I was rolling across the hall as the crowd poured out after me.

I lay there in the hall, feeling weak, which is how I realized that it was me laying there. Catskinner had retreated while I was in the air. At which point I figured I probably should get up before somebody trampled me.

Russwin was leading the crowd out, offering encouragement and instructions and in general acting like the wise and strong authority figure in the midst of the crisis. He was good at it, too. He didn't even need to point his gun at anybody.

Alice came up beside me. "Are you okay?"

"Yeah." I got to my feet. "What was that?"

"Some sort of metamorphic anthrophage," she answered absently. When am I going to learn to stop asking questions like that? "We need to get moving," she added.

I was about to ask why when the pink goo started oozing out from under the door.

"Right."

The crowd was headed down the hall to the front doors. I didn't see anybody from any of the other events—had they evacuated the rest of the con while we were in the slideshow presentation? They must have, at the same time they were putting the frames in front of the door. Whoever "they" were, they had been busy.

All for me? Sure, it was flattering, but was I really worth all this trouble? I didn't know who this Agony Delapour was—except that she probably wasn't really named Agony—but I figured she was a good reason to leave town. I should have run as soon as Dr. Klein and her goons had killed Victor.

Alice and Russwin could keep fighting the good fight. Me and Catskinner, we just weren't the world saving types. Florida, maybe. I could stand seeing the last of cold weather for a while, and I could set up shop taking out drug runners—nice, safe, human drug runners with lots of guns and cash. I'd destroy the drugs. That way I could save a little bit of the world.

One of the girls headed for the exit in front of us slipped and fell, then two others beside her. Alice held out a hand to stop me, but I had already seen them starting to liquefy. The pink goop had flowed under the other set of doors and headed back down towards us.

A smart blob. This could get *really* ugly.

Chapter Twenty-One

"that which can not go on forever comes to an end."

I turned and looked back the way we came. The goop hadn't quite filled the hallway behind us. There was room for a quick run and a short jump to get past it, but only if I moved now, so I did. As I ran I felt Catskinner's focus and heat on my back like a sunburn, but he didn't try to take over. I jumped and made it with feet to spare.

Alice kept up, more or less. I heard her hit the ground just after I did, and she kept running. The rest of the crowd—those who hadn't been dissolved—were going the other way, to the front of the building. Russwin was up there somewhere. Alice and I were cut off.

"Do you know where the back door is?" I asked her.

She was gasping. I glanced back—the goop was flowing slowly enough that I felt comfortable slowing to walk. Gratefully she fell into step beside me.

"No . . . . I didn't see anything back this way."

I looked around. Blank hallway, doors at the end. "There's got to be one, right?"

"Yeah . . . or you can punch another hole in a wall."

Maybe. Or maybe I'd drop dead of a heart attack as soon as Catskinner tried anything. But they had to have a loading dock, employees entrance, something.

Assuming it wasn't nailed shut. I found myself wondering if being turned into goo hurt.

The doors we were headed towards were labeled "No Admittance—Employees Only." Past the door the hallway continued. It was dirtier, darker. The walls and the carpet were the same, but they hadn't been kept up. A half-open door on the left led to a storeroom with mops and buckets and vacuum cleaners—and no door out. Moving on there was a door on the right. I opened it—a restroom with a tiny window way up high. Keep going.

I glanced behind me. The goop was flowing under the "Employees Only" door. It seemed to be moving faster. Alice glanced back, took a deep breath, and broke into a jog.

Another door on the right. I pushed it open. It was a kitchen— cold and dry, evidently not used any time recently. The big stainless steel tables were empty.

Except for the one that held Godiva.

I stopped and Alice ran into me.

"There's no exit here," she said breathlessly.

"You go on," I told her.

"You can't do anything for her."

I turned to her. "You. Go. On."

She nodded, started to say something, then turned to go. The door swung shut behind her.

Catskinner was silent as I walked slowly to the table where Godiva was tied down. He didn't really experience time the same way living things do, and he didn't understand that the pink goop was flowing behind us and would reach this room soon.

I did, but I didn't care. I was too tired and too hurt to care.

Godiva. She looked so small, naked and bound to the table, cut open like that. The wound was smaller than it had looked on the screen, maybe the length of my forearm, running from the bottom of her rib cage to the little tangle of soft golden pubic hair. For the picture the edges of it had been pulled apart, but they had mostly closed now, leaving only an inch or so of her insides exposed at the widest point.

There was almost no blood. I wondered where it had gone.

It wasn't right.

She wasn't human, but she wasn't a monster, not like me. She didn't deserve to be stripped and butchered and left like this.

The plastic was thick and had been wrapped around her body and the table multiple times. Somehow it made her look more naked than if they'd just left her without clothes. I fumbled one of Catskinner's knives out of my pocket—the survival knife—and slit the plastic. Peeled it off. Underneath it she felt so cold.

Alice was wrong, I could do something. I could do this. I could treat Godiva like a person instead of a thing. Maybe no one would ever know, and maybe it was the last thing I would do, but I could do it. It mattered. I looked around, but there was no trace of her clothes, or her glasses, or her teeth. I took off my shirt and laid it across her body. It covered her breasts, the wound in her belly, and her groin. It gave her some dignity.

Death happened. It was inevitable. Everybody dies, even the powerful, the wise, and the strong. Dehumanization, though, that wasn't inevitable. That didn't have to happen, and as long as there was breath in my body it wouldn't happen to anyone who had been kind to me.

Strength, I had always believed, lay in being able to do what another could not do. For the first time I encountered someone truly stronger than I was, someone who could do what I could not. Looking down at Godiva's body I realized that there was no better death than to die fighting that kind of strength.

I lay my head on her chest. She seemed warm, with the shirt over her.

That was it, all I could do. Time to go. If I could.

The pink goo was flowing under the door to the kitchen, smoothly crossing the tile floor towards my feet. As an abstract ideal, dying for a noble gesture sounded good. Looking at the reality, though, was a little different.

I hopped up on the table next to Godiva. There really wasn't room for both of us, so I cradled her head in my lap, pulled my feet up. Let's see if this shit can climb.

It pooled around the legs of the table, but stopped when it was maybe four inches deep. It filled most of the kitchen floor, but it seemed to be able to defy gravity only to a limited extent. Fatal it might be, but it still had the limitations of a fluid.

Then Godiva's body jerked. I jumped in response and damn near knocked both of us off the table. Her mouth opened and sucked in air, a long ragged breath. A moment later she exhaled. She was breathing.

She had been dead. I was sure of that—I knew all about how dead people looked and felt. Somehow, now, she was breathing, and dead people didn't do that. I had thought she had felt warmer when I put my shirt on her, and now I was sure of it. She was alive again.

I held her and her breathing smoothed out. I put my hand on her neck felt her pulse.

Her eyes opened.

"James?"

I nodded. I couldn't speak.

She reached to put her arms around me and then lay back down. "Oh . . . ow!" She looked down at herself. There was blood on my shirt now. Gingerly she reached out and lifted it to look under.

"Oh, that's not good. What the hell happened?"

"Well, um, somebody wrapped you in plastic and then started to, uh, dissect you."

She sighed and laid her head back down. "Typical." She turned her head gingerly from side to side. "Is there any of that plastic wrap left? That'll do until I get some suture."

"But—" I was overwhelmed. Too much, too fast. "You were dead."

She looked up at me quizzically. "No, I wasn't."

"Yes, yes you were. Believe me, I know dead when I see it. You were dead. No breathing, no heartbeat, cold skin, not bleeding—dead."

"I was in anaerobic stasis." Like she was saying she'd been taking a nap.

I took a deep breath, tried to force myself to be calm. "I don't know what that means."

"Oh," she reached up to take my hand. "I keep forgetting how much you don't know. I'm sorry." A pause, and I could see her trying to dumb down the explanation so I could understand it.

"Okay," she began. "You know I'm not human, right?"

I nodded.

"I was born human, and then . . . I got changed. Like you, with the servitor configuration on your back. But, in my case, it's a physical symbiosis. There's a, well, it's an alien plant life form living inside my body. It has the ability to restructure my body and it can synthesize various organic compounds—like what I fed you."

I nodded. That much I could grasp.

"Now, it's more or less under my conscious control. It responds to my brain's commands, just like the body I was born with. But it's different from me in a lot of ways. It's a vegetable, and it's a pretty damned tough vegetable. Very hard to kill. Case in point—it doesn't need to breathe."

"But you do." I objected.

"Yes and no. See, when my body—my animal body—becomes oxygen starved it passes out. But the symbiote doesn't. Instead what it does is take over the functions of my blood supply with its own circulatory system. It's an osmotic—eh, that doesn't matter. The point is that the animal part of me was in a kind of suspended animation and the plant part of me was keeping it alive. That's why I didn't exhibit any obvious vital response."

"So when I cut the plastic off your face—?"

"It let oxygen get to my lung tissue, so the symbiote was able to reactive my aerobic respiration cycle." A pause. "It woke me up."

It was incredible. She was alive. "Like sleeping beauty, only without the kissing part."

She smiled up at me. "Sometimes the dragon does rescue the princess." She lifted her hand to my face and touched my lips. "We can do the kissing part later."

She started to swing her legs around and I grabbed her. "Wait! There's more. There's some kind of flesh-eating goop all over the floor."

She craned her head to look down. "Flesh-eating goop, huh?"

"Yeah, it's like The Blob. If you touch it you dissolve and turn into more of it. Except bones—it leaves the bones. Alice called it a—" I concentrated—"meta . . . morphic anthro . . . something."

"Metamorphic anthrophage," Godiva supplied. "Yeah—that just means that it eats you and turns you into more of itself, which really is what any carnivore does, except the process takes a lot longer with most things. It's got to be a depolymerizing agent, probably bound to some simple free ranging intelligence. Where did it come from?"

"Catskinner killed this guy and he turned into slime, and the slime got a bunch of other people."

Godiva bit her lip. "Assume that it's able to metabolize at least some of the tissue as a food source . . . hmm. It left the bones, you say? They were clean?"

"Nothing but bone."

"Not good. Skin, connective tissue, muscle, hair—that's a broad spectrum agent. We've got to kill it."

"I'm in favor of that. How? I'm guessing stabbing it won't do much good."

Godiva looked around. She sat up, pressing my shirt to her belly. I winced in sympathy. "There might be something in those cabinets that can help."

The cabinets in question were a good four feet away, above the steel counter that ran along three sides of the room.

"Like what?" I asked.

"I don't know. Something. Can you get there and look?"

Could I? Catskinner could, I was sure of it, but he had been oddly quiet since he'd smashed through the wall in the meeting room.

Can you get me over there?

perhaps. there is risk of further damage to your pattern.

Risk? How bad a risk?

unweaving.

You mean it might kill me?

yes.

If I fall into that blob it will definitely kill me.

you can jump that far without me.

The hell of it was, he was probably right. It was a little far for a standing broad jump, but if it had just been chalk lines on the sidewalk I wouldn't even have hesitated.

"Okay, I'm going to give it a shot," I said. "Catskinner has been using up a lot of my . . . I don't know, chi force or something. He says that it might kill me for him to take over, so I'm going to make the jump myself."

Godiva looked at me gravely, then nodded. "I understand."

She started to twist her body to face me, then stopped, grimacing. "Be careful," she said, pain in her voice.

"Oh, yeah," I agreed. "Careful is priority one."

I got up on my knees, then on my feet, moving slowly. The table was as steady as pavement—probably bolted to the floor. I looked over at the counter top—wide, clean, probably bolted to the wall. It didn't look that far.

Then I looked down at the pink goo that covered the floor, the stuff that would dissolve me the moment I so much as touched it. All of a sudden that counter looked a lot farther away

I took a deep breath and got ready.

wait.

Yes?

bend your legs more.

I crouched a little. This okay?

and turn to your left.

I turned a little. Like this?

now jump.

I jumped. Both my feet hit the counter, and then my face hit the cabinet, but I was able to grab it. There was a moment of panic, but I was there and solidly planted. Not bad.

Thank you.

i understand how not to die.

That he did. I opened the cabinet closest to where I'd landed and started looking for things to help us not die.

Chapter Twenty-Two

"there is nothing so complete that it cannot be abbreviated."

"Let's see. Ketchup, mustard, steak sauce—oh, here we go! Salt, a ton of salt. That's got to be good, right?"

"It's not a slug, it's an animated viscoelastic liquid. Keep going." Godiva was lying back on the table, holding my shirt to her belly. I didn't like how bloody it was getting.

I went to the next one. "Plastic forks, spoons, cocktail napkins, plastic cups—no good, right?"

"Right."

The next one held more of the same. "Salt shakers, tablecloths, napkin holders, candles—"

"—wait!"

"Candles?"

"Tablecloths, what kind?"

"Uh," I poked through the stack. "Paper, plastic . . . paper and plastic, looks like."

"Gimme one of each."

I looked over at her. "You're going to kill the slime creature with tablecloths?"

A drawn-out painful sounding sigh. "No, I'm going to stop my bleeding with tablecloths, so I can live long enough to kill the slime creature."

Oh, yeah, there was that. I scooted around on the counter so I was facing her. "Okay, I'll just, uh, gently lob them, okay?"

"Paper first." She wasn't looking good at all.

191

I pulled out a paper tablecloth—in a plastic bag, so maybe it was sterile, or at least close. I tossed it and it landed on her chest.

"Thanks." She pulled my shirt off her. It was soaked in blood. "You're not getting this back. Sorry."

"I don't care about the shirt." Under the shirt she looked worse than not good. She raised her head enough to glare at me. "Keep looking."

Right. "Uh, big jars. Olives, cherries—"

Godiva let out a long gasp, tinged with pain. "Well, on the plus side, this is a really neat incision. If I can get the edges lined up—ow—it probably won't even scar."

I tried to concentrate on the contents of the cabinets. "Pickled eggs—eh, does anybody eat those? Let's see. . ." I had to scoot down the counter to the next one.

Godiva was talking, quietly, to herself. "Okay, Dr. Millerson, will you close?" Then to me, "I don't suppose you've run across a couple of tubes of super glue?"

"Sorry, not yet—"

I heard paper rustling and her body shift on the table, mixed with hisses of agony. "Rule number one, keep the insides on the inside and the outsides on the outsides. . . . Okay, toss me a plastic one, okay?"

I'd left them in the other cabinet, so I had to scoot back. I grabbed one and looked back. She was wrapped in white paper from shoulders to thighs. Red was already leaking through the front. I tossed the plastic tablecloth and she reached for it, but it slipped through her fingers and fell with a splat in the pool of flesh-dissolving goo.

"Shit! I'm sorry, I—"

Her eyes closed for a moment, then she looked back to me. "Just get another one."

I threw the second one so it landed on her. "Good, what else have we got over there?"

I scooted back across the counter. "Coffee, filters, cream and sugar, stirrers, cups—"

"No help, go on."

Plastic was rustling now. Her movements sounded slower, and her gasps of pain more frequent.

The next one was stuck. No wait— "It's locked."

"So fucking break it open."

I still had Catskinner's knives. I took the modified screwdriver and jammed it between the door of the cabinet and the frame. I leaned into it and it popped open suddenly. For a heart-stopping moment I teetered on the edge of the counter then pulled myself back up.

"Booze. Rum, whiskey, vodka—"

"Now you're talking!" The rustling paused.

"You need some to sterilize your cut?" I asked.

"Naw, I don't much worry about infection. My symbiote doesn't play well with others. It pretty much kills off anything else that tries to live in me. No, alcohol's a poison."

"It—yeah, I knew that." I looked over the edge of the counter. "So. . . how do I get it to drink?"

A choked laugh, then a gasp. "Just pour it in the goop."

That was simple enough. I started with a bottle of vodka, spun the cap off and poured it over the side of the counter. I was expecting steam to rise from it, but the clear liquid just spattered onto the think pink goop and got absorbed by it. When the bottle was empty I reached for another.

"So, how do we tell when it's dead?" I asked.

Godiva rustled a little bit in her plastic wrap. "Ah, that's better. Well, it's not exactly 'alive' now, but the chemical bonds that allow the captive outsider to manipulate the fluid require a quasi-organic stability. The alcohol should break that down—it should begin to flow downhill when the outsider loses cohesion."

I was halfway through the second bottle. "Which way is

downhill?"

"Hmmm. Well, if we're lucky there's a drain under all that goop—this is a commercial kitchen, after all."

She shifted and then sat up on the table. "Ahhh. . . . Much better. Do me a favor, use the rum last, okay? I could use a shot."

I dropped the second bottle of vodka, grabbed one of gin. "Do you think that's a good idea? What with, uh, that cut and all?"

She shrugged. Now that her body was tightly wrapped she looked much better. "I can't go into shock—the symbiote would just put me in stasis again before that happened."

The gin was gone. There were a couple of bottles of whiskey, I grabbed the cheap one first. No sense in feeding Glenlivet to the blob if I didn't have to.

"Rum's very high in sugar, you know." Her voice was starting to sound better, too. "Easy to metabolize. I used to be a beer drinker, back in school. Never had much of a sweet tooth, before. Part of the change, these days I crave sugar all the time. Of course, I don't have to worry about cavities anymore—or gaining weight, for that matter. Like you, I'm eating for two."

It turned out we didn't need the Glenlivet. After two bottles of the cheap stuff the goop started to change. The color was first, turning grayish, and then it got runnier, like an egg cooking in reverse. I watched it for a while and it was definitely flowing, slowly, towards a low spot that looked like it concealed a drain. It had lost the surreal animation and had become just a floor full of slime.

"Is it safe now?" I asked.

"Let's give it couple of minutes," Godiva cautioned. "Best not to get it on bare skin even after it's poisoned. And I don't have shoes."

"I can carry you," I volunteered. She looked at me and I added, "Me. I'm not helpless without Catskinner, you know."

you are not helpless, Catskinner agreed. *you can carry her.*

Godiva smiled at me, brushed her hair out of her face with a bloody hand, "Of course you're not, James. I'm just a little . . .

fragile at the moment. I'd rather walk."

"How about water?" I asked.

"I'd rather have rum," Godiva admitted.

"No," I pointed down, "for the stuff. We could wash it down the drain, right? It wouldn't wake it back up or anything?"

"Hmm? No, once the outsider's decoupled from the material, it degrades pretty fast."

I scooted down some more on the counter. There was a double sink, I put a stopper in one side and started it filling, then looked around for a bucket or something like one. I found a big square stainless steel dish—it looked like it fit into a steam table.

As I was waiting for it to fill I asked Godiva, "What do we do?"

"Just rinse it down the drain. It's not—"

"No! I mean about this whole mess. I can't go on like this. They're going to keep trying to kill me, and sooner or later they'll succeed, and, hell, I don't even know who they are!"

i can protect you.

"Shut up!"

Godiva was staring at me. "I didn't—"

"Not you," I pointed at my head. "Him."

The dish was full. I dumped it over the side of the sink, set it back in to fill again. The water made pretty good headway on the goop.

"James." Godiva's voice was soft.

I looked at her. She was sitting on the edge of the steel table, her bare legs dangling above the slimy floor, her body wrapped in bloody paper and plastic. She smiled at me.

"Just relax, okay?"

"Relax?" I couldn't think of any part of this situation that called for relaxing.

She nodded gravely. "Relax, and try to think. There are things that don't add up. There's more going on here than just what we see."

The pan was full again, I dumped it over the side. More goop swirled down the drain. It was starting to smell, I noticed, like meat gone bad.

"More going on?" I prompted her.

"Keith Morgan isn't the only player in this game."

"Keith Morgan!" The pan was full again, I dumped it. "Keith Morgan isn't a player in any game any more, unless it's bowling. As the ball."

"What do you mean?"

"I mean some woman in red had his head cut off and stuck in an ice bucket. She showed it me."

Godiva stared off into space for a moment, chewing her lip. "Interesting," she said slowly. Then, "A woman in red?"

"Yeah, she said her name was Agony. Agony.... something French."

"And she said she'd had Morgan killed? Did she say why?"

I thought back. "He was foolish. He tried to get Catskinner to agree to a covenant."

Godiva smiled and nodded, working out something in her head. I dumped another pan of water. The floor around the drain by the sink was pretty clear, just wet. I hopped down off the counter. I didn't dissolve.

It's the small victories that count.

"I should have seen that coming, after the bowling alley, but I was too focused on trying to save White, and then they jumped us, of course."

"White's alive, by the way," I said. "They dropped them off at the hospital."

"They did?" she seemed mildly surprised. "Morgan wouldn't have. He must have been overruled."

"Or else he was already dead by then." The pan was full again, I sluiced the water towards the table Godiva was sitting on.

"Or . . . maybe he didn't know about ambimorphs and blue metal boy. Hell, he couldn't have gotten that attack together that fast—he would have just found out the minraudim failed."

"So two different people are trying to kill me?"

"Probably more than two," Godiva answered absently, then added, "But not all of them want to kill you."

"That's good news. Isn't it?"

Godiva looked over the side of the table. "Very good news—we just have to make sure the right group wins. Help me down from here?"

Her body, under the wrapping, felt warm and soft and alive again. It felt good to have her lean against me, but I could feel how injured she was. She winced and muttered, "Fucking adhesions."

She was able to stand on her own, though, and I took a slow step back. She smiled at me. "Not so bad, really, I just have to move slowly."

I let out a deep breath that I hadn't known I'd been holding. "Good. We can go slow. What next?"

She looked around. "Let's see if I can find some clothes. They wear uniforms in this dump?"

Chapter Twenty-Three

"reality is temporary. also amusing."

When we went out the back door—both of us wearing shirts that proclaimed us employees of Endless Night Catering and Events—the lot was a mess of flashing red and blue lights. At least four patrol cars, an ambulance, a big hook and ladder truck that seemed to have no purpose except to block anyone entering or leaving the parking lot. No one was looking in our direction, so we glanced around. We'd found Godiva's glasses and teeth, but her clothes hadn't survived.

A bunch of dazed conventioneers sat around, hovered over by uniformed personnel. In one corner was a knot of arguing suits. I figured that was my best bet for finding Russwin.

He didn't disappoint me. He and Alice were both there, being lectured by an overweight man who sat on the trunk of an unmarked car, a lit cigarette burning in one hand.

"Look, I've got thirty-seven witnesses, or possibly victims, or maybe perpetrators, but what I don't have is a fucking crime. I've got statements here that there was some kind of disturbance during a presentation, and, okay, we've got some minor injuries. There was a panic, people got stepped on, it happens. Other than that, what I've got is a colossal waste of my time."

He seemed to notice his cigarette, took a deep drag, then turned to Alice. "Now, ma'am, I understand your concerns, honestly, and I want to help. But these days, I can't just pull people off the street for a psych eval unless I have some kind of evidence that they represent a clear and present danger. 'The guy looked goofy to me, your honor,' just ain't good enough. Not that I'm doubting your professional expertise, but I need to cover my ass."

He looked up as we approached the group. "And who the hell are you?" he asked, not belligerently, just exasperated.

"Ergot poisoning," Godiva said.

He blinked at that. "Okay, Miss Ergot Poisoning, what are you doing here?"

"It's Dr. Ergot Poisoning. Millerson, CDC."

"Charmed. Now we've got, what, a food poisoning outbreak? And how did I end up ass deep in feds without anybody letting me know you were going to be in my town?"

Alice and Russwin were both staring at us. Alice recovered first. "Dr. . . . Millerson. Good to see you're okay."

Russwin was still staring.

The cop shook his head. "Ergot. That's what, a poison mushroom? Makes people go crazy, right?"

Godiva nodded. "It's a fungus, usually found in contaminated grain. I've reason to believe that there may have been organic foodstuffs that contain significant amounts of contamination."

He sighed. "This crowd is certainly loony enough." He pulled a radio out of his jacket pocket. "Advise the EMTs that we may be dealing with ergot poisoning." A pause. "Ergot, Echo Romeo, Golf, Oscar, Tango. It's a fungus. Have them check for it, okay?"

He put the radio away and looked at me. "Do I want to know who you are?"

"Ozryck, DEA." I held out my hand, but he didn't take it.

"And DEA is here . . . why?"

I looked over at Russwin. "I'm on loan."

He raised his eyebrows at that. "On loan, huh"—a phone rang in his pocket—"hold that thought."

He stuffed his radio in one pocket, pulled a small phone out of another. "Clarke."

"Okay." He held up his hand—quite unnecessarily—for silence.

"Yeah. . . . I got that. . . . Right." He closed his phone and glared at each of us in turn, ending at Russwin.

"Okay, Deputy Special Agent Mister Russwin Sir, why don't you, your shrink," a nod to Alice, "your doctor," a nod to Godiva, "and your library book," a glare at me, "leave my crime scene, if this *is* a crime scene, and if it's not too much trouble, my city. In fact, why don't you all go back to Washington? Or, really, any place you like—so long as it's not here."

Russwin nodded, looking contrite. "Thank you for your cooperation, Captain Clarke. I'm sorry for any confusion."

Captain Clarke turned away without another word and began waving over some uniformed officers. We slunk away.

I was heading around to the front parking lot, but Godiva caught my arm. "Your van's over here."

Russwin and Alice were still going the other way.

"Wait," I said, "Uh, where . . .?"

"We'll meet up at your motel," Alice replied.

"Okay."

It was good to be back in my van. It didn't look like anything was missing. I could check under the spare tire for the cash I'd hidden there later.

It was good to Godiva back with me. I was kind of surprised how natural it felt to look over at her, sitting in the passenger seat, lip syncing along to the radio. I got on Highway 55, going north.

"Take 44," Godiva said.

"But the motel's off 70," I pointed out.

"We've got a stop to make first."

"Is this part of your plan?"

"Yep."

"Make sure the right one wins? Wins what?"

"The struggle for Morgan's old job."

"How do we make sure the right one wins?"

"I dunno yet."

"Oh. Well, who is the right one?"

"I'm not sure."

I drove along quietly for a while. When the interchange for 44 came, I took it, going west. I considered asking more about her plan, then decided I'd probably be happier not knowing.

How long do I need to rest before you can come out again? I asked Catskinner.

a day, perhaps.

We could stay hidden that long. Probably.

Godiva was staring out the window.

"So," I asked her, "are you really a doctor?"

"Huh?" She looked over at me. "I was. My license's not current."

"What happened?"

A sigh. "I woke up one morning and realized that I didn't want to spend my life cleaning up other people's blood and shit, and I owed too many people too much money to do anything else."

"Oh." I thought about that. "Yeah, I guess that'd be bad."

A shrug. "So when Dr. Klein offered a way out, I took it."

"Where'd you meet her?"

"I met her at the candy store. She turned around and smiled at me—you get the picture?"

"No, not really."

"Never mind. I met her at the hospital. She was a pharmaceutical rep. Heh. That was just a sideline. She was in a lot of other businesses."

"Yeah, I guess so."

"Get off at Lindbergh."

I signaled and started getting over, then looked over at her. "Where are we going?"

"The Good Earth."

That didn't sound right. "Why? Morgan's dead."

"Somebody's going to be there. We need to know who."

Did we? Did I need to know who was cleaning out Morgan's store? Godiva seemed to think that there were good guys and bad guys, and the good guys would help us. I hadn't seen any good guys, just a succession of people trying to kill me. They'd almost succeeded, too. I'd never been pushed this hard, this long. Was that the point? Was their plan to just keep sending threats at me until my body rebelled at Catskinner's control? Did they know that I had such a limit? I hadn't, not until I hit it.

All I had was questions, and no good answers. Put that way, maybe Godiva was right—at this point any information would be welcome. I felt like I was doing a jigsaw puzzle with too few pieces. And no picture on the box. Plus some of the pieces were on fire. Also every time I got a piece out of place a trap door would open in the ceiling and drop an alligator on my head.

I sighed. What's the worst that could happen?

we could die.

Everybody dies.

not everybody dies today.

We can't run forever.

we can run as long as we have to.

Not me. No more. I'm sick of running.

russwin has weapons. he will protect you while you rest.

We don't know what we're facing.

it doesn't matter what we're facing if we turn away from it.

Yes it does. They will follow us. They will find us. They will kill us.

kill them first.

Maybe Godiva can figure this out. Maybe she can make a deal.

i will not die a slave.

A different kind of deal. Some way to end the fighting.

there is no end to fighting except death.

I refuse to accept that.

I looked over at Godiva. She was watching me, her face serious. She could tell that I had been talking things over with Catskinner, I realized. "Well?" she asked.

"Let's go see who's at the Good Earth."

She smiled. "Yeah," she reached out to put her hand on my arm. "One way or another, we have to end this."

She glanced out the window, then back at my face. "Catskinner," she said softly, "I promise you that I won't let anyone enslave you or kill James. I can do things, too—not the same things that you can do, but I can keep us all safe. Trust me."

Well?

i think she is wrong, but thank her.

"He says thank you," I said.

She smiled. "Did he really say that?"

I nodded. "He also said he thinks you're wrong."

A bark of laughter, followed by a groan of pain. "Note to self: don't laugh."

"This isn't a good idea," I said. "I'm exhausted, you're cut open. Let's just go back to the hotel. We can check in on the Good Earth tomorrow."

Godiva turned to look out the window. "Pull over," she said softly.

"Where?" We were passing a strip mall, I tried to see what had caught her eye.

"Anywhere." A deep sigh. "We have to talk."

"Okay." I pulled in, found a parking place. Turned off the van. She was still turned away from me, looking out the window. I waited.

"They told me to bring you there. To the Good Earth," Godiva said without looking at me.

"They?"

"The ones that grabbed me and Alice from the parking lot.

After they separated me from Alice, but before they knocked me out. They told me to get you to the Good Earth, as soon as possible. Today, if I could."

Oh. Well, that explained that. "Did they say why?"

Another sigh. "They said that you could still make a deal. They said that they just wanted to talk."

I nodded, thought it over.

"Did they tell you not to tell me?" I asked her.

"No. That was my idea. I was going to just lead you there. But I can't."

I started the van again. "Thanks for telling me."

I pulled out of the lot and back onto Lindbergh.

Beside me Godiva murmured something. I looked over at her, she was leaning over, her face in her hands.

"What?" I asked her.

She looked over at me. "Are you going to kill me now?"

Oh, for God's sake. Now she was doing it, too. I took a deep breath. "No, Godiva, I am not going to kill you now. I'm going down to the Good Earth, and I'll talk to whoever is there."

"But—" surprise filled her eyes. "You don't think—I mean, it's sure to be a trap."

I remembered what Russwin had said. "Yeah, it's a trap, and we know it's a trap, and they know that we know, and so on and so forth. We go anyway, or we run away. I'm tired of running."

Godiva nodded glumly.

"Besides, maybe it isn't. Like you say, there's a lot about this that doesn't add up. Maybe they really do just want to talk."

"I'm scared."

"Yeah," I agreed, "Me, too. But I'm also angry. I'm sick of this shit, all these weird-ass things jumping out at me. I'm sick of being Dr. Junior Frankenstein's Science Fair Project, I'm sick of everybody talking about things I'm too stupid to understand—"

"James, you're not—" Godiva began gently.

I drowned her out, "and I'm sick of everybody asking me if I'm going to kill them all the time!" I turned to glance over at her. "I mean, Jesus, I thought we had something for a minute there. I like you. I thought maybe you liked me. I thought maybe, for the first time in my life, I might be able to get close to somebody without scaring them away. Oh, God... from the first minute I saw you, I wanted to protect you. I've been doing everything I can to keep you safe. I trust you. I thought you trusted me."

"I do trust you."

"No. No, Godiva, you do not. Because when you trust somebody, you don't FUCKING ASK THEM IF THEY ARE GOING TO KILL YOU!"

I turned back to the road. Luckily, the traffic was light, my eyes were blurry. I blinked and felt tears on my cheeks.

"I'm sorry." It sounded like she might be crying, too.

"Yeah." I took a deep breath, got my voice back under control. "There's a lot of that going around."

We drove on in silence for a few blocks.

"I do like you, James. It's just . . . I've had kind of a rough week," Godiva said.

I looked back at her and she flashed me a brave little smile. I smiled back, and it felt good.

"Fair enough," I said. "It hasn't been easy for me, either." I held out my hand to her.

Her smile got bigger, and she took my hand. "I promise, on days that I don't have my abdominal wall incised I'm not nearly so irritating."

That made me laugh, and laughing made some of the tension flow out of me, and made me realize just how scared I was, and how fear made me lash out at everyone, even the one person I was sure I didn't want to hurt.

Godiva laughed, too, even though it made her wince.

Laughing, we pulled into the lot of the Good Earth.

The white pick up truck was still the only vehicle in the lot. I wasn't sure what, if anything that meant. I parked the van and wiped my hands on my jeans.

How do you feel about this? I asked Catskinner.

i don't like it.

Me, either. I got out of the van. I heard Godiva getting out of her side, and turned to her.

"You don't have to—" I began.

"Hush," she said, "I'm going with you."

I didn't argue. Instead I opened the door to the shop and the three of us went inside.

Chapter Twenty-Four

"and they all lived happily every after. until they died, of course."

The bell above the door rang flatly as I pushed it open—odd, I didn't remember that from the last time I'd been here. The view was the same, though. A shelving unit directly ahead, filled with a random selection of stuff. I turned right into the spiral, Godiva keeping step beside me.

The same confusing mishmash of stuff on the shelves, wind chimes and mirrors and charcoal briquettes and energy drinks without any order that I could see. Godiva frowned at the shelves as we passed, nodding now and again, as if she was working out the filing system.

Me, I was much more concerned with the figure in the center of the spiral maze. There was a figure standing there, I could tell that much through the shelves. It was moving, picking things up or putting them down, sorting things on the counter, maybe. It didn't seem to have noticed us, but it was hard to tell because what I could see of its head seemed strange, over sized.

A turn, a turn, a turn, past paperbacks in some Asian language and cheap automotive tool kits and stacks of paving stones. Beside me Godiva muttered, "Feng Shui on steroids—"

"Huh?"

"This place is an energy trap," she explained softly. "By placing opposing elements across from each other he channels energy—

chi—into the center of the spiral. It's really quite clever."

And I thought he was just a lousy merchandiser.

The figure in the center of the spiral didn't seem to take any notice of us. There was something just wrong about the silhouette I glimpsed through the shelves.

What is it?

it is a collection of decay.

Which made me wonder if Catskinner could even see the figure in the middle or was just talking about the crap on the shelves.

We had reached the center. I held out my hand to stop Godiva—whatever was here, I wanted to encounter it first.

It was Keith Morgan. With a little portable TV where his head should be.

"Well . . ." I said. "This is revolting."

a collection of decay.

Yeah, I could see that. Morgan's body didn't look good—even more than just the whole missing head thing. His skin was pale and dry and his flesh seemed to sag, somehow, like it wasn't his muscles holding him up but some kind of interior framework. There was dried blood crusted all around his neck and spattered across his T-shirt—this one showing some pink-haired busty anime character.

There were . . . things . . . running from the bottom of the TV and into Morgan's neck—wires and tubes and metal struts. To avoid looking at them I looked up at the screen. It showed a face. It was the woman in red—Agony Delapour.

That figured.

Godiva came around me and stopped, staring at the altered body. She looked at me. "Yeah, that is revolting."

She looked back at the figure. "So . . . I guess you're the new boss?"

On-screen Agony laughed. "New? Oh, no, I've always been the boss. This—" the arms of the body moved to indicate Morgan's torso"—was just a useful idiot."

"He seemed to think otherwise."

Agony turned her head to face me through the screen. There had to be a camera somewhere in that mess of tubes and wires, but I didn't want to look for it. "Of course he did—he was an idiot. Which is what made him useful."

"But his usefulness came to an end," Godiva suggested.

Agony shrugged. "It happens." A sigh. "There's a lot to be said for letting one's underlings think they're in charge, but the downside is that sometimes they just won't do as they're told."

"And then you need a new idiot," I said.

Another laugh. Her laugh was bright and cheerful just as if she wasn't speaking through a remotely operated desecrated corpse. "Fortunately, there's no end to those! The only way to approximate infinity, you know."

"And I suppose that you think you're in charge?" Godiva asked sharply.

"On my good days. Now, Godiva, I see you brought Adam to me, thank you so much."

"Actually, I brought myself," I pointed out. "Godiva told me about your conversation, and I came of my own free will." It seemed very important for me to say that. "Also, don't call me Adam. It's not cute any more."

"She just trying to get under your skin," Godiva said.

"No, not really." On the screen, Agony looked down, as if she was looking at the body under the TV. "Now, Mr. Morgan, his skin I got under."

I'd had about enough of this particular freak show. "Okay, I'm here. What do you want?"

"Well, first I wanted to apologize for all the trouble you've had lately. Really, none of it was my idea."

I wasn't buying it. "The last couple of things that tried to kill me were after I met you and you told me Morgan was out of the picture."

Agony sighed. "Yeah, I know. If you attack people, they tend to defend themselves. But it wasn't anything you couldn't handle."

"You cut Godiva in half. Or are you going to claim that wasn't you, either?"

Agony shrugged. "Don't exaggerate, she wasn't cut in half. But yes, that was me—well, I gave the order. I had to get your attention. I wasn't expecting you to react quite so . . . intensely."

"Intensely?" I was starting to react intensely again. I took a deep breath and tried the reign in my emotions. "I thought she was dead. How did you expect me to react?"

"I admit that I expected you to know more about ambimorphs, since you'd taken up with one. But leaving that aside"—Morgan's body made a limp slash with one hand, mimicking an airy wave—"I certainly didn't expect you to become so attached to one that you'd just met."

"Obviously you don't know a damned thing about me."

"I know everything—" Agony began angrily, then stopped. Her face on the screen looked straight at me, the image of her eyes met mine for a long moment. "Maybe you're right. It seems I was wrong about that, anyway."

"Look, is there a point to this discussion? Because I'd really like to get home, take a shower, get some sleep."

On screen Agony leaned forward. The body mimicked the action, flopping its arms down on the counter and lurching to a leaning posture. It made me notice what was on the counter—little clear plastic boxes filled with. . . bugs? But Agony was speaking again.

"I don't believe you really understand the position you are in," she said, doing her best to look serious and concerned.

I shook my head. "Tired, hungry, and scared. Same position I've been in all my life."

"No, James, listen to me," Agony continued. "There are things happening that you don't understand."

"Yeah, it's been like that my whole life, too." I turned to go. Enough was enough.

go back and listen to the construct.

That shook me. I paused.

Godiva touched my arm. "I think we need to hear this."

Okay, I was outvoted, two to one. I turned back around. "Fine," I sat down on the floor, my back against a shelf. "So explain it already."

Godiva look at me sitting on the floor and sat next to me, her side warm against me. She took my hand. "Where do we go from here?" she asked Agony.

The body held up a hand. The effect was spoiled by the fingers hanging limply. "That is the big question," Agony said. "You have to understand—"

Godiva cut her off. "What if James had accepted Morgan's offer from the beginning? Would any of this be happening?"

Clearly Agony wasn't used to being interrupted. "Not as such, no. We would be having this conversation eventually, but not under these circumstances."

"What conversation?" I burst out. Godiva and Agony turned to look at me. I sat up a little straighter, shrugging away from Godiva. As much as I loved snuggling up against her, she was starting to annoy me, too.

"I mean, a conversation—if I understand the concept—is when two or more people exchange information, right?" I continued. "Like, Person A says, don't open that door, and Person B says, why not? and then Person A says, because there's a giant exploding scorpion-bat behind the door that will fuck your shit up, and Person B says, gee, thanks, I won't open the door—that, that would be a conversation!"

"James—" Godiva began. Agony just stared at me.

I kept ranting. "What's been happening to me lately has not been conversations. What's been happening is that people make bizarre enigmatic little comments in my general direction, and weird crap comes out of nowhere and tries to kill me. And then when I say, hey, how come weird crap keeps coming out of nowhere and trying to kill me? everybody tells me I don't understand what's going on. Newsflash, people—DUH! I know I don't understand what's going on. I was there when the lack of comprehension was happening."

I took a deep breath. My eyes—damn them—were all blurry again. I blinked a couple of times, felt tears on my cheeks. Godiva put her hand on my arm and I lurched to my feet. Stepped away from her. I didn't want her touch, not right then.

"Okay, I get it—I'm stupid. I have figured that much out. So explain using little words. Start with why Morgan wanted to kill Victor and keep going until you get to why you are using him as Mr. Potato Head for Psychos."

"James," Agony began, "It's—"

"So help me," I shouted her down, "If you say 'it's not that simple' I will . . . I will . . . I don't know what I'll do, but it'll be bad. And ugly. And there will be lots and lots of blood."

On the screen Agony opened her mouth. Closed it. Blinked a couple of times. Morgan's body just kind of hung there.

"Okay," Godiva began. "I'll start—feel free to jump in any time, Red. Morgan killed Victor because Victor wouldn't cut him in for a piece of his action. Victor thought he could get away with being an independent because he figured Catskinner could take out any enforcers that Morgan sent. Am I doing okay so far?"

Agony frowned, but nodded. "Essentially. It's not—it's a little more complex than that."

I glanced over at Godiva. "And Dr. Klein?"

Godiva shrugged. "She was looking to get out of town and out of the business. Taking Victor out was the price."

I nodded. That was basically what Dr. Klein had said.

"Morgan figured the Solomon trick would kill me, right? Or did he just not care?"

I looked at Godiva. Godiva looked at Agony. Agony frowned.

"That is troubling," Agony said slowly. "I suspect that the orders he gave Dr. Klein were to kill you. Presumably pity stayed her hand."

"I don't know," I said. "He didn't seem that surprised to see me. And he had that water thing all ready to go when I didn't take his offer."

Agony shrugged. "He had a whole stable of bound demiseraphim."

"Airish beasts. That's what Catskinner called them."

"Now, when did you kill Morgan? After he sent the minraudim?" Godiva asked.

"Those were the fire centipedes, right?" I asked her.

She nodded, looked back at Agony.

She nodded. "It was clear he was off-track. I ordered him to relinquish control of this nexus, he refused." A shrug.

"So you cut his head off," I frowned, "Then who sent the metal man and the strippers?"

"I have no idea," Agony said simply. "Honestly. William was a freelancer. He recruited Dr. Klein's former staff himself, without telling them who he was working for." Agony turned to face Godiva, the body lurched sideways a bit. "You know how ambimorphs are about concealing information."

A bitter chuckle from Godiva. "Yeah. Not exactly masters of deceit." She sighed. "Where are the girls now, anyway? Did you kill them, too?"

Agony looked hurt. "Kill them? Please, why would I waste such a resource? No, they are happy and healthy and working. Mostly here, but I did send some of them to Vegas." A smile. "That's an offer still open to you, by the way, little darling. I assume that the, uh, physiological effects of the symbiote are the same, even though the psychological shift seems to be less severe than with most of your sisters."

"I did a residency in neurology. I suppose that I could visualize what the symbiote was doing in enough detail to influence it to leave my frontal lobes alone." Godiva stood. She was moving much more comfortably than she had been earlier. "Sometimes I wish I hadn't."

"The burden of self-awareness," Agony said ironically.

I thought that over. So Godiva was the same kind of . . . ambimorph that seduced all those people at the bowling alley. It made me wonder what she would have done if I had accepted her offer back at The Land Of Tan.

Best not to think about it. Evidently she was different from the others—smarter. But she had probably been smarter than most people before the symbiote, too. Maybe that's why Dr. Klein left her in the shop.

"Those guys outside the bowling alley?" Godiva continued.

"Those were mine," Agony continued. "And I am sorry about the incision. It does seem to be healing nicely."

Godiva ran her hand over her belly and nodded. "Probably not even a scar." A glance over to me. "They wrapped me first, so I was unconscious when they cut me."

"Well," I said. How do you reply to something like that? "I guess that was considerate. The dinosaur and the blob?"

"They were simply supposed to lead you here. But once you attacked them. . . ." Agony let her voice trail off.

I rubbed my head. "Okay, so now I guess I make a deal with you, or you kill me. Isn't that how things work in your world?"

"James." Agony's voice was very serious. "Look at me. I promise to you that I will not kill you, nor will I give the order that results in your death. There are those who want you dead, though—you and Catskinner both, and Godiva because she associates with you. I want to help you. I can help you much better if we work together."

I looked at her, and I looked at what she was using to talk to me. "You know, using the dead body of an ex-employee as a puppet isn't real great for your recruitment."

Godiva nodded. "He's got a point. I can't help but wonder what promises you made Keith Morgan."

A toothy grin from Agony. "I never promised I wouldn't have him decapitated." The grin faded away. "He attacked me. Not directly, and it's possible he didn't understand the implications of his actions, but it was an attack nonetheless. In my position, I have to respond to threats unequivocally."

"What is your position?" I countered.

Agony frowned at that. Maybe she considered direct questions to be crude, uncivilized. Too bad.

"I consider myself to be a dealer in inequities," she said at last. Huh?

"Is Morgan's job still open?" Godiva asked suddenly. My question had given Agony pause, Godiva's made her stop altogether, staring coldly from the monitor for an uncomfortably long time. Godiva waited.

"What, precisely," Agony said slowly, "do you think that Morgan's job was?"

Godiva ticked off the points on her fingers. "One. Communication. Relaying information, messages, orders, from one group to another in a form that they can understand and accept. Two. Disinformation. Ensuring that no . . . enhanced individuals come to the attention of the general populace and taking steps to plug any leaks, if and when. Three. Logistics. Managing the flow of outsider-produced goods in and around the area and stockpiling them against shortages. Four. Security. Keeping knowledge of your existence on a strict need-to-know basis." A flash of a grin. "How am I doing?"

"You have my attention." Morgan's body folded its hands, sloppily. "Go on, make your pitch."

I wasn't sure I was comfortable with where this was going. "Wait a second—"

Godiva held up a hand to me for silence. I shut up.

What's going on? I asked inside my head, not really expecting an answer.

perhaps safety.

Godiva was talking, choosing her words with great care.

"The primary risk of operating through an agent is that the agent will attempt to usurp you. In order to do that the agent has to believe two things. First, that she or he doesn't need you. Morgan believed that because the ones he dealt with saw him as the person in charge—they reinforced what he wanted to believe about himself. That's not an issue with me. Look at me. Even with James as my enforcer, no one is going to believe that I'm the one calling the shots. Consequently, I'm not likely to start believing it."

Agony considered this, nodded.

Godiva continued, "They won't know who is pulling the strings, but they will be sure it's not me. That's safer for me, too—makes me less of a target."

"And the other thing?" Agony asked.

"The agent has to believe that it's possible to cross you and get away with it." Godiva looked down at her abdomen significantly, then over at Morgan's body. "That is not a mistake that I will ever make."

I couldn't keep quiet any longer. "Are you seriously considering working for her?"

Agony answered me. "Yes, she is. And I am seriously considering accepting her for the position."

"But—" I didn't know where to start.

Godiva took a step towards me and reached out her hand. "James, trust me. We can make this work. You've got the brawn, I've got the brains."

it is an elegant solution.

I nodded.

"You do realize that there will be challengers? With Morgan gone, there will be those who want his network," Agony pointed out.

Godiva shrugged. "Let them have it. Better yet, let them fight over it." She looked around the shop. "Not much here I want. You let Morgan work for you and think he was king of this town. I figure letting someone think he's king of this town who isn't even associated with you is a better cover still."

Agony smiled. "I like how you think."

Godiva smiled back. "I want Alice Mason and Cobb Russwin on my team. Would that be a problem?"

Agony shook her head. "Not at all. Subcontract what you like, so long as the work gets done."

Godiva sat back down, looked up at me. I sat beside her and she took my hand. It felt good.

"Now, let's make a deal."

the end

About the author:

Misha Burnett has had little formal education, but has been writing poetry and fiction for around forty years. During this time he has supported himself and his family with a variety of jobs, including locksmith, cab driver, and building maintenance.

Catskinner's Book is his first novel. The basic idea came from a desire to create a new mythos, to set a novel in an entirely new Urban Fantasy world, without vampires, werewolves, zombies, fairies, or any of the standard fantasy tropes.

Major influences include Tim Powers, Samuel Delany, William Burroughs, and Phillip K. Dick.

More information about upcoming projects can be found at http://mishaburnett.wordpress.com/